ASSORTED CONUNDRUMS

ASSORTED CONUNDROMS

THE SPADE/PALADIN CONUNDRUMS

NOVELS

Ten Little Fen

COLLECTIONS

The Early Conundrums

Assorted Conundrums

SHORT STORIES

"Stomping Mad"

"The Case of the Vanishing Boy"

"The Karnikov Card"

"Pandora's Box"

"Trick or Treat"

"The Really Big Ka-Boom"

"At Witt's End"

"Unity Con"

"The Case of the Stolen Memories"

"The Case of the Purloined Pages"

ALSO BY KRISTINE KATHRYN RUSCH

THE DIVING SERIES

Diving into the Wreck: A Diving Novel

City of Ruins: A Diving Novel

Becalmed: A Diving Universe Novella

The Application of Hope: A Diving Universe Novella

Boneyards: A Diving Novel

Skirmishes: A Diving Novel

The Runabout: A Diving Novel

The Falls: A Diving Universe Novel

Searching for the Fleet: A Diving Novel

The Spires of Denon: A Diving Universe Novella

The *Renegat:* A Diving Universe Novel

Escaping Amnthra: A Diving Universe Novella

The Court-Martial of the *Renegat* Renegades: A Diving Universe Novel

Thieves: A Diving Novel

Squishy's Teams: A Diving Universe Novel

The Chase: A Diving Novel

Ivory Trees: A Diving Universe Novel

Maelstrom: A Diving Universe Novella

THE RETRIEVAL ARTIST SERIES

WRITING AS KRIS NELSCOTT

THE SMOKEY DALTON SERIES

A Dangerous Road

Smoke-Filled Rooms

Thin Walls

Stone Cribs

War at Home

Days of Rage

Street Justice

AND

Protectors

ASSORTED CONUNDRUMS

A SPADE/PALADIN COLLECTION

KRISTINE KATHRYN RUSCH

In Memory of Mike Resnick

CONTENTS

INTRODUCTION

In the years since I started writing the Spade/Paladin stories, the world of science fiction has changed. The conventions faded in importance in the past ten years. Social media is partly to blame, as are—oddly enough—comic conventions which grew dramatically. And then there was a massive internecine fight in sf that destroyed goodwill on both sides.

All of this occurred before the Covid-19 pandemic which put a stake in the heart of some conventions that had been marginal anyway.

I had been struggling with the changes in sf as I wrote three of the stories in this volume.

I struggled harder when I wrote *Ten Little Fen*, the only Spade/Paladin novel so far, partly because so many of my friends in the field had passed away. The afterword for that novel lists the members of sf fan- and pro-dom who had left the planet by the time of that writing, and I had to keep updating it before publication date.

If I were to update it now...well, jeez, as I put this volume together, I lost one of my mentors, Michael Bishop, a man who taught at my Clarion Writers' Workshop in 1985, and who wrote some amazing, amazing works. Just this weekend (as I write this), another longtime fixture in the field passed away.

The deaths are almost weekly now, because the sf fans and pros that I "grew up with" have aged. And, to be honest, sf people have never been physically healthy, so many of them die young.

I still grapple with how to write Spade/Paladin stories and remain true to the fun of them. Mostly I straddle the old world and the new. I have to acknowledge many of the good changes, but I do miss the old world as well. I had been very active in that world for twenty years, and I want to honor it.

So now, the world that Spade and Paladin inhabit is not the world of today. It's not the world of yesteryear either. It's their world. That realization has freed me to write several new stories in the past few years.

I've collected them here. The first Spade/Paladin collection, *The Early Conundrums*, had five stories, so I wanted five in this as well. The problem was I only had four uncollected stories.

Which meant I had to write a new one for the collection.

And I did.

That story is "The Case of the Purloined Pages." It surprised me a great deal. It's more of a writerly story than a fannish one, but that's all right. Writers are a big part of the sf (and mystery) universe and deserve their due.

Writers also make an appearance in "Unity Con" and not in the best way. I wrote that in the middle of that internecine struggle, and it's reflected in there...just a bit, anyway.

"At Witt's End," is a tribute to my friend Bill Trojan, who loved the Spade/Paladin stories. He would be happy to see the series continue. But he was one of those people who probably would not have a place in modern sf. He had a difficult personality, one that forced him to anger people often and on purpose to see if they were worthy of friendship. If they got mad at everything he said, he ignored them. If they laughed and gave as good as they got, they became friends.

Considering how politically incorrect he was back in the day, he'd probably be considered toxic now. (And justifiably. I can't tell you how many times I had said, "Biiiilll," in a disapproving tone, just to get him to shut up.)

Yes, I miss him. And dozens of others who lacked social skills and found a refuge in sf. I'm not sure that particular refuge still exists, except inside of the Spade/Paladin universe.

When I wrote "The Case of the Stolen Memories," evoking yet another friend who shall remain nameless, I reminded myself that internecine fights were not unusual in sf.

The sf convention movement was born in the middle of one of those fights, which happened around the 1939 Worldcon—the first Worldcon, in which the fighting got so severe that some of the founding members of fandom locked other founding members out of the venue.

The parts about that Worldcon and First Fandom (minus the crime elements) that appear in "The Case of the Stolen Memories" are all true—including the very sad reality that some members of First Fandom never ever forgave other members. The fight continued for decades.

Oddly enough, that reassured me and enabled me to return to Spade and Paladin's world in "The Case of the Purloined Pages."

There are more Spade/Paladin conundrums to come. Of course, since I write into the dark, I have no idea what they will be. I'm not even sure if they're short stories or novels. I just know that they're like an empty table at a science fiction convention, waiting to be filled with old friends.

—Kristine Kathryn Rusch
Las Vegas, Nevada
December 11, 2023

THE REALLY BIG KA-BOOM
A SPADE / PALADIN CONUNDRUM

"Do you have plans for Christmas?" I asked Paladin, and then flushed. I couldn't believe my own boldness. I felt like Stalker Spade.

I hadn't planned on running into Paladin here, at one of the Los Angeles megamalls. In fact, I hadn't planned on seeing anyone I knew. Everyone I knew in Los Angeles (well, not everyone, but almost everyone) was at a hotel near LAX, celebrating Black Friday the way that sf fans always celebrated Black Friday—at a science fiction convention, with hundreds of their closest friends.

Paladin was an sf fan, but she didn't make conventions the center of her life. Nor did she make malls the center of her life. I only knew bits and pieces of her life, the bits and pieces she let me know over the short time we'd known each other.

Mostly, what I knew about Paladin was that she rescued people. She took her inspiration (and her business card) from the old *Have Gun, Will Travel* TV show. She's a wanderer who digs into whatever crisis she can, usually those involving kids.

I had no idea she was going to be in Los Angeles, let alone at this mall. I had seen her before she had seen me, which was kind of amazing, considering this was one of those big Los Angeles malls that made product placement a god, and people watching difficult. Plus there had to be a thousand people here, most of them in the broad walkway between the shops.

Paladin isn't very tall—5'4" on a good day—but she has a distinctive look. She's thin and elfin, with upswept ears that end in a point. A man who is not involved with a woman should never have a favorite part on that woman's body, but I do have a favorite when it comes to Paladin. Those ears sold me the moment I first saw her. They were real, unlike most pointed ears you see at science fiction conventions, and they fit her puckish face.

I've seen a lot of fake pointed ears. I spend my life at science fiction conventions—literally. I am a Secret Master of Fandom, which sounds grand, but actually means I'm one of a group of people who make sure that science fiction conventions all over the world go off without a hitch. Fans call us SMoFs (pronounced "smoff") for short, and only those fans who truly pay attention know who we are.

"Christmas?" Paladin said drily, as if she couldn't believe I'd said that. "I'm working."

Her sarcasm carried over some Bing Crosby wannabe's hideous version of "White Christmas." I resisted the urge to close my eyes and smack myself in the forehead with the heel of my hand.

I had been thinking of Christmas—who didn't in this environment?—and then I saw Paladin. I'd been talking to other fen (that's the real plural of "fan" in the sf world), and we'd been trying to figure out who was coming to Chinese Food Con.

Chinese Food Con wasn't a real convention, but it was what we called our annual holiday celebration. Actually, we had two celebrations. Chinese Food Con was for those fen who didn't celebrate Christmas. Started by Jewish fans decades ago back when the only restaurants open on Christmas Day were Chinese, Chinese Food Con lasted five whole hours and usually ended at the screening of some major holiday movie at a designated multiplex. After a while, we even started moving Chinese Food Con from town to town, picking the best or the most accommodating Chinese Restaurant in the area.

Chinese Food Con was one of my favorite traditions. I hadn't missed in years.

I often missed the second holiday tradition: Regifting Day. The fen had been doing that long before regifting even became part of the lexicon. Usually held around New Year's, again in a designated city, Regifting Day had strict rules. The regifted item couldn't be cool. It had to be the worst gift you got that year.

Since I didn't get many gifts (some years I didn't get any), I had no reason to attend Regifting Day, even though I had heard it was fun.

So when I saw Paladin, heard the Christmas music, saw all the red-and-green and exhausted crowds, I asked her what I'd been asking everyone I liked at the convention. *Want to join me for Christmas?* sounded so normal when asked of casual friends at an sf con.

It sounded creepy and vaguely weird in the middle of Black Friday celebrations at one of the biggest malls in the country.

"I know," I said, "I figured you were working. I wasn't inviting you to my house or anything. It's just we have a tradition in fandom for Christmas Day and I wasn't sure if you knew about it, and—"

"I'm *working*," she said again, with unusual emphasis, and I nodded like the doofus I was.

Of course she was working on Christmas. I'd never known Paladin to do anything except work.

3

Not that I was one to talk. I wasn't at this mall for a Black Friday reason. I was here for a convention reason.

A phalanx of Klingons who had come here to scare the civilians had left behind a small troop who had started playing some light saber game in the center of the mall. Yes, yes, I know the irony of Klingons playing a Star Wars game, but most mundanes don't, and they crowded around as if they were watching the second coming of the *Enterprise*.

One of the Klingon leaders had to be on a panel at four, so he rounded up the bulk of the team and left. When they got back to the hotel near LAX, they sent me into deepest darkest Los Angeles to save the rest of their people from the mundanes.

"Well," I said, sounding even dumber than I usually did around Paladin, "in case your job cancels or something, we have this fannish tradition from the deepest darkest days of prehistory. It's—"

"Where's Chinese Food Con being held this year?" she asked as she peered around me.

My entire face was on fire. I didn't know how I could screw this conversation up more.

"Um, Oregon. Portland. There's this great restaurant near the tram that someone found at last year's Orycon, and we decided that it would be spectacular for this year's—"

"Fine, good," she said, and then she pushed past me.

I turned, just to say something else, like maybe goodbye or I'm sorry or something profound (in my dreams), but all I managed to see was Paladin's back as she slipped into the crowd. She looked like one of those heroines from the cover of an urban fantasy novel, all boots, muscle-shirt, and leather. She just needed a broadsword over her shoulder to complete the image.

The crowd swallowed her, and I was left alone with my terminal embarrassment.

At that moment, a Klingon clapped his steel-gloved hand on my shoulder and said, "Kapla!"

I was so startled, I almost stammered, *And may the Force be with you too!* but I managed to avoid that faux pas. Still, I didn't feel like answering in Klingon.

"You guys ready to go home?" I asked, and as he nodded, I realized that I didn't even have to apologize for the word "home." We both knew what I meant, and we both knew the truth of the word.

For us, an sf convention truly was home.

———

I didn't see or hear from Paladin again, and I figured she'd forgotten our encounter. Actually, I *hoped* she had forgotten that encounter. I wished I could.

I went to SMoFcon the following weekend, and presented two panels on accounting for sf conventions. Most people don't realize that conventions are multi-million-dollar enterprises, and must be handled the way that large businesses are handled. That's the reason I get called into most conventions; someone has messed up the books (again), and I have to fix everything.

After SMoFcon, December slows to nothing, which is why non-religious fen who consider conventions their home feel a bit lost at this time of year.

I do. I retreat to my house in Seattle, do the obligatory maintenance, sort through everything I bought at the various conventions through the year, make sure my own accounts are in order, and try to go out at least once a day.

I don't work. I'm what's called in Northwest parlance, a Microsoft Millionaire—one of the early Microsoft employees who got paid in stock options as well as ready cash. Mine vested back when Microsoft was the biggest company in the world, and I made millions. Unfortunately, most of my Microsoft Millionaire colleagues handled money the way that brand new sf conventions do, and those folks aren't millionaires any longer.

I know how to handle my funds, and even after all the economic ups and downs of the past few years, I've still quadrupled my original take. I probably would have made even more, except for the holiday season. I believe in the charitable giving thing; I know a lot of folks who are struggling, and they get a visit from a Secret Computer Santa who pays off their house or their credit cards or their one and only car. There's usually a tree and wrapped packages involved too.

It still means I spend the bulk of the holidays alone.

I have a personal tradition: I show up for Chinese Food Con about a week before (depending on frequent flyer blackout periods), and explore the city. Every city has different traditions for Christmas, and each one is both familiar and unfamiliar at the same time.

Even though I live close to Portland, I'd never been there over Christmas. I stayed downtown—not in one of the trendy boutique hotels, because I'm not a trendy guy—but in one of the high-end chains that had been downtown forever. I've stayed in so many hotels that I'm more at home in them than I am in my house, and I expected things—24-hour room service, enough TV channels to keep me entertained, a functioning bar, and access to a concierge who doesn't look down his nose at a 350-lb man in an *X-Men* T-shirt.

On December 23rd, I went down to the bar for some hot wings and a microbrew. I had gone to local concerts on all of the previous evenings, but there were none tonight—or at least, none I wanted to attend, since most were in churches.

I was thinking of dinner and a movie. I had my iPad out to see

6

which films were showing, and try to figure out which the Chinese Food Con folks wouldn't want to attend. That ruled out all the sf movies, of course, and left me with the hopeful (and possibly dull) Oscar contenders. I had just stooped to reading reviews when my phone rang.

"Where the hell are you staying?"

It was Paladin, and she sounded grouchy. I actually pulled the phone away from my ear and looked at the screen. Yep, the screen image was a photo I'd taken of Paladin the summer before when she was sitting cross-legged in my gigantic con chair, looking both impish and Buddha-like.

I put the phone back to my ear. "Um, why?"

"I figured you'd be at the Other Hotel, like you usually are, but it's gone. I mean, *gone*."

The Other Hotel was a joke from Portland's best convention, Orycon. Back in the day, the convention was held in a Red Lion hotel near the Columbia River. Across the parking lot (literally) was another Red Lion. People always came in and asked for something, only to be told it was in the other hotel. When Portland hosted Westercon in both hotels, the con committee actually made T-shirts that read, *It's in the Other Hotel*.

Since Orycon's standing committee was so very competent, I never had to work the convention, so I would go to relax and I would stay in...you guessed it...the Other Hotel.

"The Other Hotel's still there," I said. "It was the old Orycon hotel that burned. And I didn't know you when I stayed in the Other Hotel. Did I?"

I felt awkward. Orycon had left the complex more than a decade before. How could I have missed Paladin?

"So where are you?" she asked, completely ignoring my question, which made me nervous all over again. She had sought me out for our very first case together, which I call "The Case of the Vanishing Boy," although she doesn't like the fact that I name cases. Had she been watching me long before that? If so, why?

"Where are you?" I asked.

"I'm at the Other Hotel, I guess," she said. "Why won't you tell me where you are? I thought you always came to Chinese Food Con early."

I frowned. Had she been spying on me? I knew I hadn't told her about Chinese Food Con before.

"I'm downtown." I told her the name of my hotel. "What's going on, Paladin? Is something—"

And at that moment, my phone beeped at me, like it did when a call got severed.

I set it down and stared at the screen. Paladin had come here? After our discussion in Los Angeles, I had thought she wouldn't show up at all. She hadn't said anything. She never contacted me, and I didn't see her at Loscon (or SMoFcon for that matter). Plus, she was two days early.

I pushed aside the microbrew—I needed all of my wits about me—and ordered a Diet Coke. (No jokes, please. I happen to prefer the taste.) I ate the hot wings and wiped off my fingers. By the time I had popped in a Listerine strip to help with my breath, Paladin came through the hotel's main door.

And she wasn't alone. Beside her was her younger doppel-ganger, Casper. Casper was thirteen going on fifty. She wasn't related to Paladin at all. Casper's parents had abandoned her in the middle of the recession, and she'd ended up at a shelter. Paladin met her there, and then introduced her to me.

Casper might look like Paladin, but she had math and computer skills that made me seem like a slacker. She helped Paladin solve a case back in October, and Paladin convinced me to sponsor Casper at a private school for the totally brilliant. I paid her tuition, yes, but I also vouched for her, and that meant I got weekly reports.

They were stellar.

Still, I hadn't invited Casper to join me over the holidays. I have to be careful to avoid the creepy unrelated sick-o uncle thing with a preteen girl. Not that I have designs on anyone under thirty, but I don't want the perception to hurt either of us.

"Hey," I said to both of them as I met them near the door.

Casper, who was wearing a parka despite Portland's forty-degree temperatures, looked around. "*This* is where you spend Christmas?"

It did have upscale, somewhat inoffensive decorations, and Christmas music by actual musicians, but it didn't seem very homey.

"This is my first Christmas in this hotel," I told her.

"Expensive taste." Paladin made a face as she headed to the reception desk. She was wearing a winter version of her usual outfit—tight black jeans and layers. Ever larger long-sleeved T-shirts covered each other. I could see a hint of a tank top underneath it all. She didn't wear a jacket, but at least her black boots were practical.

She pulled a wallet out of her back pocket as she leaned against the reception desk. By the time I got to her side, she was tapping a credit card on the desk. I couldn't see the name on the card. I knew it couldn't be Paladin, but I didn't know what her real name was.

No one did—at least in my circles.

"Let me get this," I said. "My treat."

She glared at me. "I didn't come here so you could pay."

"I know," I said, and I was tempted to let her pay for the entire thing, just so that I could see what her real name was.

"I was going to find you after we checked in. But I was having a hell of a time." She still tapped that card, even though I had my black American Express card clutched in my pudgy fist.

She peered over the desk. So far, no one had shown up to check her in.

"In fact," she said, "the Other Hotel wasn't even my first choice. I went to the Beaver Motor Lodge, but left after fifteen minutes because *no one waited on me.*"

She said that last bit louder than she said the rest of it. I grinned. I wonder what she had done to try to get someone's attention at the Beaver Motor Lodge. Paladin called herself a bulldozer, and had, in fact, hired me in the past for my ability to finesse things.

She was in impatient bulldozer mode here, and I'd have to shut her down soon, but bulldozer mode might not have seemed out of place at the Beaver Motor Lodge.

The Beaver Motor Lodge wasn't really a motor lodge. It was a funky hotel in one of the areas of Portland waiting for urban renewal. The "beaver" part wasn't because of what you might think either. The beaver is Oregon's state animal, and the name of the sports teams from Oregon State University—something I always thought of as bad planning, especially for the girls' teams called (no, I'm not making this up) the Lady Beavers.

The Beaver Motor Lodge had been the site of one of Portland's latest conventions, an anime/gaming/urban fantasy hybrid called MotoLoCon. MotoLoCon (short for Motor Lodge Con) died an ignominious death when the treasurer of MotoLoCon 2 ran off on the con's first night with all of the funds. I investigated that one, found the stupid embezzler who had run all the way to Vancouver, Washington (across the bridge from Portland), and who had gone on a shopping spree at a rather downscale mall.

She was serving time, and the entire concom was not going to work conventions ever again.

I always liked Beaver Motor Lodge and thought it had potential to be one of Portland's great boutique hotels, even if it wasn't set up to be a convention hotel.

"She kept telling me how cool it was," Casper said, hands shoved deep in the pockets of her parka. Her jeans were ripped and her tennis shoes had a hole in the top. Looked like new clothes were on the agenda for this trip, whether she knew it or not.

"You don't think so?" I asked.

"Dead moose heads in the lobby? Are you *kidding* me? Ugh. And that stuffed bear was just *gross*."

I grinned at Paladin, but she didn't notice. She was peering over the desk again. No one was waiting on her here either.

"I'm never going to get a room anywhere, am I?" she said.

I hit the bell, and a man dressed in a shiny black suit appeared as if he'd been summoned by demons. The only thing that spoiled his wealthy look was the name tag on the lapel.

"These two need a two-bedroom suite," I said.

"We do not," Casper said as Paladin said, "Spade, no."

"And put it on my bill," I said before turning to them. "It's the holidays and you should be comfortable. My treat."

"I don't want a treat," Paladin said.

"Merry Christmas," I said.

"Spade," she said, not letting it go. "I—"

"Say 'thank you,' Paladin," I said.

She pursed her lips. "Thank you," she said clearly reluctant.

"You were supposed to say, 'Thank you, Paladin,'" Casper said, doing a perfect Gracie Allen. I had no idea how a kid like her even knew who Gracie Allen was, considering George Burns' wife had died in 1964.

Paladin glared at her, and I was instantly grateful they would have the privacy of their own bedrooms. Paladin didn't strike me as someone who shared her personal space well.

"She was promising me dinner at some diner near that creepy motor lodge," Casper said. "Said it had the best hot turkey sandwiches on the planet. Then we didn't stop. I suppose this place doesn't have hot turkey sandwiches either."

Clearly she was in the mood for them. And now that she mentioned it, so was I.

I smiled. "I remember that diner. It's fantastic. And it's not very far from here, if you don't detour to Jantzen Beach where the Other Hotel is."

"Really?" Casper said.

"Really," I said. "Let's just get you guys settled in."

———

It didn't take long. They didn't have much luggage. I was beginning to think Casper didn't have much of anything. Paladin wouldn't think of buying Casper clothes—Paladin was not a girl-girl—and the money I sent for expenses probably went to books and gadgets instead of necessities because Casper wasn't a girl-girl either.

I didn't want to ride in whatever vehicle Paladin had rented, so we took my Lexus SUV across the Hawthorne Bridge to the east side of town.

Fortunately the diner was open, which was more than I could say for the Beaver Motor Lodge. No cars parked in its lot, even though lights were on in most of the rooms.

The Lodge resembled a hunting lodge crossed with a motor lodge. Rooms spread out like spider legs across the parking lot, but the bulk of the lodge went up four stories in a rickety wood building that looked like a sneeze could knock it over.

No one had even bothered to put up Christmas decorations.

Apparently the Beaver Motor Lodge was on its last legs. Too bad. I had enjoyed the place when I stayed there.

The diner, on the other hand, thrived. We didn't have to wait in line, but only because the place was huge. A waitress in a 1960s brown uniform and matching beehive hairdo grabbed three gigantic menus and led us to a table near the window.

Christmas music was playing here too, but era-appropriate: Elvis singing about his ba-ba-ba-blue Christmas and the Safaris (I think) doing a surfer rendition of "Jingle Bells." The decorations that the Beaver Motor Lodge lacked were out in force here, from plastic lights nestled against real evergreen along the frosted windows to little Santa suits on the ketchup bottles. If you were not in the spirit of the season, you did not belong here.

I think Paladin was the only one who glanced at the menu. Casper and I wanted hot turkey sandwiches, and we ordered them, along with corn bread and soup and a bunch of other stuff neither of us would probably eat. Paladin finally decided on a cheeseburger.

We had just gotten our drinks when the world went black and white and whump! all at the same time. I got blown sideways out of the booth, landing on a vibrating floor.

Sound hit me next—a ka-boom like I'd never heard before. (And in my stunned mind, I kept hearing Marvin the Martian repeat in his little alien voice, *A really big ka-boom!*) It *was* a really big ka-boom, followed by another really big ka-boom, and yet another.

Sleet landed on me, at least, I thought it was sleet until a piece landed just in front of my nose.

Broken glass.

Heat rolled over me, which I thought was very weird, and then a hand grabbed my arm, pulling me away.

I looked up.

Paladin, her face covered in blood, elfin eyes big, saying, "Jesus, Spade, I don't want to drag you *and* Casper. Help me here."

She had Casper by her arm. Casper looked dazed, but not out. She was getting to her feet.

I almost said, with the impeccable logic of a man in shock, that Paladin wouldn't have to drag both of us, and then I realized that Paladin couldn't drag me any more than she could stop a moving train. I mentally imbued her with supernatural powers because she was the most fascinating person I had ever met, but that didn't mean she actually had those superpowers.

Somehow I got to my feet, terrifyingly unalarmed by placing my hands on glass shards to boost myself up, or the fact that the booth wasn't anywhere in sight, or the way that the blood was dripping off Paladin's lovely skin.

In addition to Marvin's really big ka-boom voice, another voice in my head calmly and rationally reminded me that shock had its virtues but a realistic assessment of the danger around a person was often not one of them. Yet a third voice told me that it was winter, and heat shouldn't roll in the window.

I listened to that third voice, put my arm around Casper to move her forward, and let Paladin tug us both to the back part of the diner. As we moved, so did other people. They were screaming or crying or searching through debris.

Paladin was telling them all to get out, get out, and asking for cell phones so that someone would call for help. But she kept moving all the same, and we got to the back of the building—which was intact. I wanted to stay there, but Paladin made us file through the door leading to the alley—not just me and Casper, but all the people huddled there.

"Stay away from the building. It's not stable. And wait for me," she said before running back inside.

I thought—stupidly, but all of my thoughts in that crisis were stupid—that I had finally met someone who would run into a burning building, and it didn't surprise me that that person was Paladin.

"She gonna be okay?" Casper asked, holding me so tight it would have hurt if I could have felt any pain.

The fear in Casper's voice caught my loopy brain and somehow focused it. I held her close. This poor kid had lost everything the past year, and had somehow stayed strong, and now she was going through this. If she lost Paladin too, she might break.

So I did the cowardly thing: I spoke with extreme confidence as I lied.

"Of course, she'll be okay," I said. "She's Paladin after all."

————

And she was a paladin that night, one of the foremost warriors in the world. She battled heat and smoke and fires, broken tables, and collapsed ceilings to get at least fifty people out of that building. I did what she told me to do: I moved everyone away from any walls that could fall, and kept a tight hold on Casper who was using the new iPhone I sent her three days before it got released to repeatedly call 911 and yell at them for not sending anyone.

She sounded so outraged and so strong that I didn't want to inform her that someone was on the way: we were just in time dilation, as they would say in *Star Trek*. Everything was happening in slow motion, at least to us. Seconds became minutes, minutes became hours. We probably were outside without help for fifteen minutes maximum, but it seemed like days.

And through all of those days, Paladin kept bringing injured people out, and going back in for more.

Her layered shirts were ripped down to the tank, her jeans were in tatters, and the blood on her face had turned black. Or maybe it was just covered with so much smoke and dirt from the flames that it looked black.

She didn't stop even after the fire trucks arrived, and she didn't curse them the way that the crowd did, when they went across the street.

That was the first time I looked up, and saw what was really going on.

The Beaver Motor Lodge was gone, from its four-story center to the tentacles spreading across the parking lot. The buildings on either side—and by that, I mean across the street, like the diner on the north side, and something else (a strip club?) on the south side, had collapsed as well, and they were burning.

Fire truck after fire truck after fire truck arrived: I had no idea that Portland had that many fire trucks. As ever more arrived, I began wondering if any city had that many trucks and if I was seeing double (or triple or quadruple).

Paramedics had moved a lot of the people Paladin saved, sorting them as if they were damaged collectibles and someone had to grade them: Fair, Very Fair, Good. The folks in Mint condition stood to one side, and those who were judged Poor had already been stuffed into ambulances and driven to nearby hospitals.

Someone grabbed my arm, but I shook him off. I didn't want to be graded or placed in line. But the arm-grabber was persistent.

"We need to check you out, sir," he said softly (or maybe it wasn't soft; I was beginning to think my hearing was damaged), "and your little girl too."

It was the thought of Casper that moved me to the ambulance, and let them poke and prod me. I figured if I let them poke me, they could poke Casper too. All she kept doing was asking after Paladin, but no one knew who Paladin was.

Finally, I said, "The little woman who keeps carrying people out of the restaurant."

"Oh, her," the paramedic said. "No one can stop her."

I nodded. That about summed her up.

Casper was okay except for some cuts and bruises (Very Fine), but they wanted me to go to the hospital to treat me for shock. They also wanted to make sure I hadn't damaged anything else, which I finally realized was code for *he's fat and out of shape; he might have heart issues.*

I made them wait until they could stuff Paladin in an ambulance too. She didn't go willingly. I finally told her that I needed her to come with me, and then she sat quietly at my side, letting the paramedic check her blood pressure along with mine, search her skin for burns (miraculously there were none), and make her promise she'd get all her cuts stitched up.

The paramedic wiped off her face to find the cuts, and that was when we all realized that she was covered in ketchup. Her face was surprisingly unhurt, even though she had cuts elsewhere, especially on her hands.

"You guys sure know how to throw a Christmas party," Casper said as they wheeled me into the ER.

Paladin smiled at her and said, "We like to start our holidays with a bang."

———

I was okay. Well, as okay as an obese man who never left his favorite chair could get after he'd been flung across a room by the force of a blast that the news called (with hyperbole, of course) the equivalent of a five-megaton explosion.

Whatever that explosion had been, it had been dramatic, and by the time the hospital set me free (hanging onto me longer than expected, mostly to keep Paladin there so the docs could check her for all kinds of possible damage), it was nearly nine. We hadn't gotten our roast turkey sandwiches, and I don't think any of us were interested.

We went with the old standby. Pizza, delivered to Casper and Paladin's suite. Because I wanted to rebel against all of those nasty medical assumptions, I made sure at least one pie was a five-meat combo with extra cheese.

The suite was lovely and so not-sf conventiony. Lots of high-end furniture, real flowers, and bowls of fruit everywhere. Complimentary Champagne "for the lady" and an entire assortment of chocolates "for the young lady." Plus free big snuggly robes that Casper immediately crawled into. She looked as lost in hers as she had in her parka. But at least she was grinning.

I made the mistake of telling them about my Marvin the Martian moment, and Casper subsided into a sea of giggles, stopping only to imitate Marvin herself, and mutter, "A really big kaboom."

It did sound funny when she said it.

The local news featured the explosion, sending clueless reporters to the scene. The reporters had to stand blocks away with the still-burning fire as a backdrop. By the last newscast, someone had gotten their hands on cell phone footage of the actual explosion, and it was impressive.

Even our giggler fell silent. Paladin and I glanced at each other, clearly astonished that we had survived it.

I wanted to tell her how impressed I was with her actions, but every time I tried, she shut me down.

"You'd've done the same if you hadn't fallen so hard," she said, but we both knew it wasn't true. Give me a computer screen filled with numbers and I can tell you if they're legitimate or not. Give me a burning restaurant filled with people, and my mind conjured Marvin the Martian who, even in a cartoon emergency, wasn't the most efficient of characters.

"How come you guys aren't out there solving this?" Casper asked.

I looked at my bruised self, so big it didn't fit into the complimentary robe. I wore a loose sweatshirt and a pair of sweatpants that I usually used for relaxing around my hotel room when I was alone. I didn't look like a man who could solve anything.

And Paladin's hands were wrapped in gauze, because the doctors didn't want her stitches to get infected.

But Casper was frowning at us. I was going to ask if she noticed that we weren't really up to snuff, but Paladin—the bulldozer—spoke first.

"Arson investigation is very specialized," she said with a calmness that surprised me. "I don't have the expertise, and I don't think Spade does either."

"What makes you think this is arson?" Casper asked.

Good question. I wished I had thought of it myself. My brain was still sluggish from the day's events.

Casper glanced at the TV as Paladin glanced at me. She had a help-me-with-this look.

"I mean," Casper said, "they're saying it was a gas leak."

Paladin frowned. Apparently she wasn't thinking clearly either, or she would have answered a bit less directly.

"Remember that video of the explosion?" she asked.

I frowned, and wished the TV in the room came with a DVR. Then we could have rewound the footage.

"The explosion went through the building, and out through all of the rooms equally. If it had been a gas leak, the explosion would have been uneven, particularly in the rooms in the parking lot. They were too far away for anything but collateral damage, not for the original explosion."

Paladin used her hands as she explained this. She didn't seem like she was in pain at all. I felt like I'd been hit by a two-by-four (or maybe several two-by-fours), but she seemed physically unaffected.

"It sounds like you do know arson investigation," Casper said.

"I know logic," Paladin said.

"So you think someone set this," Casper said.

"I think someone facilitated the explosion," Paladin said. "Proving it will be hard."

Casper frowned, then she looked at me. "We should be pretty mad about this, shouldn't we?"

Bruises, no turkey dinner, the loss of the diner. Maybe we should have been mad. But no one died in the diner or in the buildings near the Beaver Motor Lodge, even though it would take some time to say for certain if anyone died in the motor lodge itself.

"I don't know," I said. "It seems to me that we're pretty lucky, all things considered."

"Maybe." Casper sounded like she was getting wound up. "But you know, Paladin and I were there for like hours. What if we hadn't given up? What if we got there later? Their front door was unlocked, the lights were on, and we were just waiting for someone to check us in. And no one did. And Paladin got annoyed so we left. But what if we didn't? We could've died."

I glanced at Paladin, who had actually paled. She hadn't thought of that.

"I didn't smell rotten eggs," she said to me. All natural gas companies tinged their product with the stench of rotten eggs, so that you knew you had a gas leak in your furnace the moment it happened, not when—you know—the entire thing blew up.

"That's something we need to tell the arson investigators," I said. "But it can wait until tomorrow."

I was exhausted. Casper had deep circles under her eyes. But she seemed to have a lot of energy.

"I know you can't investigate the crime scene," she said to me, "but I watch TV and I read a lot, and isn't arson always about insurance money?"

"No," Paladin said. "Sometimes it's about revenge or sheer—"

I gave her a look that shut her down. Casper didn't need to know about the kind of people who would burn up someone they hated simply for the pleasure of it.

"What are you saying, Casper?" I asked.

"I'm saying you know how to use computers and you are this financial wizard, and couldn't you find this stuff faster than the police?"

I took the last piece of the five-meat pizza. I think Casper had one slice. The rest had been all mine.

I tended to eat when I was nervous. I didn't remember inhaling that pizza. I must've been beyond nervous.

"I could," I said, "but anything I found wouldn't be legitimate. If this is arson, they're going to want to follow an evidence trail that leads them in the right direction. And the right direction is one that holds up in court."

"But they won't even know where to look," Casper said.

Something in her tone made me set the piece of pizza down. "And you do?" I asked.

"Well, der," she said, as if I were the dumbest person on the planet. "I mean, how coincidental is it that every hotel in Portland that holds an sf convention has burned down this year?"

"Not every hotel that holds an sf convention has burned," Paladin said, in what I'm sure she thought was a soothing tone.

But I frowned. People got ideas from other people. And the initial news reports about the old Orycon hotel fire mentioned arson. People linked to those old news reports on Facebook and fan sites as they discussed what great memories they'd had at Orycon back when the con was held in those hotels.

I know, because I wrote some of those posts. We talked about the great centrally located restaurant and how a disabled friend convinced the hotel to put in elevators to its function space and how the filking never managed to bleed into the dealer's room despite the proximity of the space. We talked about a lot of things, but mostly how sad it was that the hotel had devolved from a beloved space to a place where transients lived and fires happened, maybe for the money.

"Crap," I said.

"What?" Paladin asked.

It felt like my brain had returned. "Casper's right," I said. "This is a connection the police might never make."

"What connection?" Paladin asked.

My brain *had* returned. It was moving faster than other people's on money matters, just like it always did.

"The convention connection," I said, "and the ties Beaver Motor Lodge had to the guys running MotoLoCon."

I knew about it because I had offered to help with the books, and no one let me. The MotoLoCon people assured me they were getting a fantastic deal because one of the concom's cousins owned the lodge.

The fannish connection was slight, but it existed. And people in fandom were bright, endlessly inventive, and sometimes a bit too invested in their own abilities.

Such as their ability to remain undetected.

"I need my computer," I said as I stood up. I was a bit wobbly, but I wouldn't let myself catch the side of the couch to show weakness.

"What can we do?" Paladin asked.

"Nothing yet," I said. "Let's just see if I have reason to be suspicious."

Then I went back to my room, and got to work.

About two hours in, someone—Paladin, probably—called room service and got me Red Bull, coffee, Diet Coke, and all kinds of weird looking appetizers. The room service waiter showed up expecting a party, I guess, and seemed stunned when he realized I was alone.

I didn't really care. I did remember to tip him, and then I went back to my computer system.

I hadn't brought my tower of terror—I only used that at conventions—but I did have two different laptops, both the latest from their various manufacturers. I also had some software I designed that made it a lot easier to investigate someone's finances.

I didn't have a court's permission to dig into the finances of the Beaver Motor Lodge, but I didn't need one at first. I went all the way back to the material that one of the Oregon SMoFs had provided me about MotoLoCon.

The SMoF wanted to know if the various Oregon science fiction societies would be liable for any of MotoLoCon's debts, since MotoLoCon was using all the sf societies' good name and stellar reputation to get help with its financing.

I remembered that as a dicey case, with lots of potential problems. I scanned everything to remind myself, and then saw my e-mail back to the SMoF.

This is something we worry about if and when MotoLoCon goes belly up. If someone blames your organization, I'll be right there to prove you had nothing to do with the convention.

I had a lot of good, legal information right in front of me, and I had a reason—besides a growing need to punish someone for nearly killing Paladin and Casper—for digging through all the records.

I dug a little further, and then I turned on the news. The local early morning shows mentioned arson in connection with the Beaver Motor Lodge's demise.

That was all I needed. I picked up the phone and called an old fannish friend who had gotten transferred to Portland's FBI Bureau. He greased a few wheels for me, so that I could talk to the right investigator.

I called him—a guy by the name of Ernie Reston—and he asked to see me right away.

Apparently the FBI connection—and my impressive forensic accounting résumé—caught his attention.

———

I knew better than to show up in my usual outfit of T-shirt and jeans, but I considered it, just to emphasize my fannish cred. Instead, I hauled out my suit. I traveled with it everywhere and wore it only when I was being official.

Portland's Central Police Bureau was downtown, not too far from my hotel. I would've walked, but my bruises from the night before had turned into aches so profound I felt empathy with Oz's Tinman. I definitely needed oil in my joints. Or something. I felt bigger and achier than usual.

The Bureau was in a large stone building that also housed the Justice Department. It was impressive; I had to walk farther than I wanted to in order to get to the press room, which was where Reston wanted to meet me. I was just happy we didn't meet in an interview room; that always indicated something was about to go south.

I found a table and was just setting up when Reston came in. He was a dumpy guy whose suit fit worse than mine did. His face had streaks of soot, and he smelled like smoke. He looked so exhausted that I began to regret thinking I was tired at all.

We didn't even exchange pleasantries. Instead, I explained how I'd been asked to investigate a science fiction convention a few years ago, and what I had found.

It wasn't a lot—just enough to bend the rules in a way that would've made me hire a different group to run the convention—but in light of the fire, it looked truly suspicious.

Because MotoLoCon never made money, even though it had minimal expenses and "free" hotel access due to the cousin. The "free" access turned out to be less than free; most of the money from MotoLoCon 1 went to taxes, fees, and "additional expenses" provided by the Beaver Motor Lodge. Tens of thousands of dollars worth.

"Ballpark it for me," Reston said. "I've been inhaling smoke all night and I've been thinking about burn patterns, not financial patterns."

"Let me state that I don't have information showing what Beaver Motor Lodge did with its money," I said, "but I can tell you some of the taxes charged don't exist, which makes what I have here something the Feds are going to want to see."

"No kidding," Reston said.

"The rest of it tells me that MotoLoCon was set up to make money for the people involved, even though the corporation running the thing had filed for nonprofit status. That means the organizers could pay each other a small wage, but they weren't entitled to any profits from the convention. So they just funneled the money to the motel instead."

"And this is tied to the investigation how?" He rubbed his face, covering it with more soot as he did so.

I explained Casper's idea about the two convention hotels. Then I reminded him that criminals often took inspiration from each other to design a scam.

"Plus," I said, "I think this one little convention alone shows a pattern of financial irregularity, and a willingness to bend the rules for financial gain. With your permission, I can look into the motel's finances. Or you guys can just check to see what kind of insurance policy the place had."

"Already did," he said. "It's large, considering what a dive that was, but that doesn't mean anything if we can't prove arson."

I smiled at him. "I have some friends whom you might want to talk to," I said. "They spoke to the police at the scene, but they were at the motel a few hours before it blew. They didn't smell anything, and you'd think, with a gas leak that big, they would have."

His eyes narrowed. Then he nodded. "I would like to talk to your friends as soon as I can."

———

I took him to see Casper and Paladin at the hotel. I figured they would have more credibility in that setting than in a police setting. But I didn't have to worry. Reston had already heard of the heroic Paladin, and how she had saved countless lives.

For a few minutes, I thought she'd flee the room. Paladin doesn't do compliments well. But he saw her face, and quit. Then he listened to their story about the Beaver Motor Lodge's reception area.

And then Paladin, without any help from me, found that cell phone footage on the news station's website, and showed him how the explosion looked suspicious to her.

He eyed her sideways, then smiled for the first time since I met him.

"Yeah," he said, as if he were talking with an equal. "The rooms off the parking lot all had space heaters—filled with oil. And not the kind the manufacturer usually provides. Plus adjoining doors between all the rooms were, somehow, left open."

"I *knew* it," Casper said, turning toward me. I put a hand on her arm. Too much enthusiasm at the moment was unseemly, particularly in light of all the injuries and damage. "We'll have to testify, won't we?"

He gave her a soft smile. I hadn't known a man like that was capable of such warmth, particularly considering all he'd been through.

"It depends," he said. "I'm hoping the bastards are going to realize how hopeless this all is, and take a plea."

———

They did take a plea. But that was months and lots of attorney's fees away. Plus fees for me, because the Portland Police Bureau decided that I could continue my investigation. As expensive as I am, the Bureau didn't mind. The insurance company footed the bill. They figured it was cheaper than paying out.

It was.

But that was all in the future.

After Reston left, we decided to go out in search of hot turkey sandwiches. He recommended a few places and Paladin volunteered that any restaurant recommended by a cop had to be good.

She was right.

I had changed back, deciding on a nice holiday T-shirt, featuring Santa giving Chewbacca a boatload of gifts. Most of my other Christmas T-shirts had a lot to do with rather gruesome Santa death scenes or very obscene reindeer games. After the 24 hours we'd had, neither seemed appropriate.

In fact, the 24 hours inspired me to be a bit more forthcoming than usual. After we got our sandwiches, but before we dug in, I said to Paladin, "I was a little surprised that you showed up for tomorrow's Chinese Food Con."

She frowned at me. "You invited me."

I felt that flush return. "I did. But you said you were working."

She stared at me like I was a total idiot, and then she started to laugh.

"Spade," she said. "I *was* working. That day. In the mall. And you were screwing up my op."

"Oh," I said.

"Wow," Casper said. "You guys give a whole new meaning to socially challenged."

Paladin glared at her, but I laughed. Casper had a wicked talent for the truth.

"No matter what," I said, "I'm happy you both came."

Paladin's expression softened. "Merry Christmas, Spade."

Casper lifted her water glass and said in a perfect movie Tiny Tim accent, "And God bless us, every one."

UNITY CON

A SPADE / PALADIN CONUNDRUM

When Paladin called to ask for my help, I was sitting in a planning meeting with some fen at an ancient Holiday Inn outside of Garland, Texas. We were crowded around a fake wood conference table so old that it had cigarette burns in the laminate. We were in a calm discussion about the best way to handle hotel negotiations when my cell phone rang.

The fen—fannish lingo for a gathering of true fans—all recognized my ringtone.

It was "The Ballad of Paladin," from the old Richard Boone TV show, *Have Gun, Will Travel*. Paladin took a lot from that show, including her business card, which read:

Have Gun
Will Travel
Email Paladin@paladinsanfrancisco.com

Of course, Boone's card read "wire Paladin," but you get the idea. Paladin was a fan, even though she rarely admitted it.

And the fen in the room were savvy enough to realize from the ringtone alone who was calling me.

Paladin and I had become quite a team. When some cons had problems, they even asked for us together, which pissed her off. She preferred to work alone.

She would probably be upset at the ringtone. She had given me her cell number just a few months ago. She was stingy with information. Even though we had worked together half a dozen times, she had yet to tell me her real name.

I excused myself and went to the dusty hallway, with its sun-faded red carpet, sneezing once before answering the phone.

"Hey, Paladin," I said cheerfully, even though I knew this wasn't a personal call. Paladin rarely called me for personal reasons. Most of those reasons had to do with Casper (no, not her real name either), an utterly brilliant girl we had co-sponsored at one of the best boarding schools in San Francisco. (Long story.)

Paladin didn't bother with hello. "Where are you?"

"Near Garland," I said.

"Texas? Oh, good," she said, even though she didn't sound all that thrilled. "How long will it take you to get here?"

Typical Paladin. She thought I kept track of her. Much as I would have loved to, such behavior was called stalking and was against the law.

"Where's here?" I asked.

"Unity Con," she said.

The very name put my back up. The folks running Unity Con had irritated me from the start. I'm a SMoF, just like all the fen in that run-down conference room. We're known as the Secret Masters of Fandom for a reason. We run conventions, which are multimillion dollar organizations, and we do it smoothly.

But SMoFs had nothing to do with Unity Con. It was being

run by a group of writers who thought they knew how conventions should operate, rather than how conventions *did* operate.

These know-it-alls started their convention in response to some political ugliness going down in the professional writer community. These know-it-alls were going to show the rest of us how *inclusive* conventions should be run—forgetting, or perhaps never realizing, that fandom had always welcomed everyone. From the differently abled to people of color, fandom has always kept its doors open.

Of course, the Unity Con dreamers had run into trouble from the start. And Millie, a con organizer from the Southwest, had called me to rescue them from some kind of connish problem a few months back.

Because the Unity Con people were so damn obnoxious, I had said no.

I was beginning to worry that decision was coming back to bite me.

"You know," Paladin was saying, "they're holding the con at a stupid ranch outside of Amarillo."

I did know that. The con organizers had commandeered one of those giant Texas hunting lodges beloved by politicians and the very rich, thinking it would be a draw for the Right Kind of Science Fiction fans.

Most of the fen I knew *hated* the idea of some isolated Texas ranch. Fen liked cons in an area with a choice of restaurants, from super cheap to exceedingly high end. Some nearby shopping didn't hurt either, as well as easy access to public transportation.

"I thought you would be here," Paladin said. She sounded off. Paladin never sounded off.

"Too political for my blood," I said. "Besides, the concom is a bunch of idiots."

"Oh, you have no idea," she said. "Garland to Amarillo, what, six hours? Get here as quickly as you can. I need you."

Paladin had said that to me only a few times before. *I need you* had never quite been in the way I'd hoped, not that I ever told her what I hoped. Honestly, I hoped she never knew that I pined for her, because I was embarrassed by it. I wasn't the kind of guy a woman like Paladin would be interested in, and I knew it without ever being told.

When Paladin said *I need you* to me, she meant she needed Spade and his investigative abilities, not me and my schoolboy crush. Spade is my fannish name, which my friends had given me after I solved my first convention crime. (I always felt that Nero Wolfe would have been more accurate, since I'm six-six, four hundred pounds, and set in my ways.)

"Are you okay?" I asked, because I couldn't help myself.

There was a moment of silence. I could imagine her face. Her expression probably flattened, and she rolled her eyes just a little bit. If Casper were beside me, she would have whispered, "Are you freakin' kidding me? You're talking to *Paladin*."

And Paladin wasn't going to answer a stupid question. So I asked the question I should have led with. "What's going on?"

"They're talking murder," Paladin said.

I nearly dropped my phone. "At a science fiction convention?"

I couldn't keep the shock from my voice, even if I had wanted to. In all of my years in sf, and with all of my knowledge of the history of the field, I could not recall murder *ever* happening at an sf convention. Fen die at conventions all the time—we're not the healthiest lot—but we don't kill each other.

"Jerkwad's dead," she said. "I need you here. *Now*."

And then she hung up.

Jerkwad, dead, at a science fiction convention. At that moment, I thought things could get no worse.

I was wrong.

———

I had known Jerkwad since he had been a skinny teenager named John Johnson. The first time I met him, I was working registration at an early Dragoncon. He had shown up at the desk, with the word *Jerkwad* written in the area that asked what his name badge would say.

Jerkwad was so young, so thin, and so pimply faced that I assumed he didn't know the customs of our people. I figured he would want a better name.

So I explained that people would be calling him jerkwad all weekend, and added that maybe, just maybe, he would want to set up a different alter ego, his game avatar, or a favorite fictional character, perhaps.

He laughed, a squeaky nasal sound that reminded me of a cat about to puke, and said in the loudest voice imaginable,

"Hey, everyone! This fat turd who calls himself 'Spade' thinks I should change my name to a fictional one. You ever read any Sam Spade, turd? You're not blond and bony. You don't look 'rather pleasantly like a blond Satan' to me."

I wasn't sure what took me aback more—the viciousness in his tone or the fact that he could so accurately quote the first paragraph of *The Maltese Falcon* where Sam Spade was first introduced.

"Or," the kid continued in his nasally little voice, "have you somehow confused yourself with Bogie? Because he was a short little asshole with intelligent eyes, not like you, *Spade*."

The entire registration area grew quiet. No one had ever seen anything quite like it, at least not aimed at me.

Unfortunately for Jerkwad, I had learned how to deal with assholes decades before our little encounter.

"If you're going to take the moniker Jerkwad," I said calmly, "you really should try harder to be original. Most mundanes attack my size and my name. I expect a better, more articulate, and to-the-point attack from someone coming to an sf con."

I handed him his badge.

"Have a nice convention," I said.

He looked at it as if it had bitten him, which it kinda had. Because I had spoken loudly too, and it sounded like I was the one who had given him his nickname.

I had also called him a "mundane" which was an insult to a hardcore sf fan.

And I had done both in the silence of first-day registration at what was slowly becoming one of the biggest science fiction conventions in the nation.

He never shook the perception that I had given him the nickname, which irritated the hell out of him. He didn't like me, so he didn't like the fact that I got credit for something as important as his con name.

Usually guys like him vanished the moment they left adolescence. But he didn't. He gained professional credentials. He published his work in well-known (excellent) European venues and some truly dodgy venues here in the States.

He moved to Europe, joined some nasty political movements (there were rumors he was a Neo-Nazi), and attended a few European cons. Mostly, though, he hung out on the internet. He found all its dark corners and assembled minions of hatred to do his bidding.

It didn't hurt that he was literate and funny and could write better than most of the people who criticized him. Reading his takedowns of other people was always entertaining even while they were appalling.

Even though the politics of science fiction fans veer from libertarian to ultra conservative to liberal to progressive, most fen don't go after each other for their views. Jerkwad did. He attacked anyone who wasn't as right wing as he was. Worse, he did it the way he had attacked me, by commenting on people's appearance or their greatest weakness—the way that bullies in the real world did.

Those bullies were the reason most of us had fled to sf in the first place. We tolerated a lot of socially inept speech in our community, but overt bullying was something that got moved out of the sf convention circuit in very quiet ways. Concoms, at least those staffed by SMoFs, simply did not allow the worst bullies to return. Suffering the pain of bullying was, after all, something we all shared, and we didn't want to replicate it in our safe place.

Then, a few years ago, the entire sf community got torn apart by a fight over politics in the community's highest award, the Hugo, and Jerkwad was in the middle of all of it, egging people on.

He started to come back to conventions in the States after that, invited by people who agreed with his politics.

And that, apparently, was how he ended up at Unity Con.

When I turned Unity Con down months before, I had no idea they had invited Jerkwad. Maybe they hadn't then. Not that it mattered. They had, and he was dead, and some things were never going to be the same.

———

I went back into that grimy conference room and asked if anyone knew where I could rent a helicopter or private plane.

"They're calling you to Unity Con?" someone asked.

I felt the blood leave my face.

"We know," said a long-time fan who had called himself Groot after the 1960 *Tales to Astonish* villain. (Not the popular *Guardians of the Galaxy* character, but his predecessor). Groot was small, wiry, and ageless. He was wearing a blue-and-white checked shirt and bolo tie, even though he wasn't from Texas. "Dave got a text."

Dave was another SMoF, like me. Only unlike me, he didn't use a con name. He was tall, like me, but unlike me, he was too thin. He also had a beard that was as long as it was unruly.

"I'm heading there now," Dave said. "You want to come?"

I did not want to spend the next six hours in a car with Dave. I liked him, but we couldn't converse on any single fannish topic without coming to violent disagreement.

"I have a plane," Groot said, saving me from answering Dave. "I can call and get us in the air in less than thirty minutes. I'll have a pilot standing by."

His offer did not surprise me. Groot wasn't the first fan to have his own plane. I had toyed with the idea myself, given how much I traveled. But it was a lot cheaper to rent the occasional private plane and fly first-class the rest of the time than it was to keep my own plane on standby like Groot was doing.

"It won't take long to get there at all," Groot said. "That ranch is set-up for Presidents and ex-Presidents. There's a landing strip that'll handle Air Force One if need be."

"Okay," I said. It looked like we were going to travel in style, at least. "I have a few things to get from my rental car, and then we can go."

As we headed out of the hotel, I dialed Millie, the friend who had first contacted me about Unity Con.

"You at Rancho Cielo En La Tierra?" I asked.

"To my everlasting regret," she said. "I told them not to bother you. You said you wouldn't come near this place."

"Yeah," I said. "Another friend called me and told me about Jerkwad."

"We have it handled, Spade," she said, her tone flat. That was when I realized she was mad at me for refusing to help with Unity Con.

"I'm hearing talk of murder, Millie," I said.

"You know how fannish rumors work," she said.

"I do," I said. "I also know that the person who contacted me doesn't gossip. Ever."

Millie swore softly under her breath. Dave, Groot, and I had reached my car. I put her on hold for a moment while we decided if I should drive.

They dithered, so I made an executive decision and slid into the driver's seat.

Then I took Millie off hold. I decided I wasn't going to argue with her anymore.

"I need rooms for Groot, Dave, and me," I said. "*Separate* rooms. We'll be there in the hour."

"We don't have rooms in our block anymore," she said.

"You have a block at a dude ranch?" I asked, and the other two looked at me, their eyes wide. "Level with me, Millie. The ranch is empty except for all of you, right?"

"We're not paying for more rooms," she said.

"Oh, yes, you are," I said, and hung up.

———

It took us two hours to get to the ranch. We spent some of that time scurrying through near-rush hour traffic in Garland. The rest of the time we spent—unhappily, at least on my part—in the air.

Turned out Groot's idea of a private plane and mine were two completely different things. Mine was Lear Jet with a steward and snacks. His was a six-seater developed in the Johnson administration with its last tune-up about the time Jimmy Carter became president.

I barely fit in the damn thing, and I could barely tolerate it. Texas air is full of turbulence, and I felt like I was on a malfunctioning ride at a cheap carnival in some backwater out of Ray Bradbury's *Something Wicked This Way Comes*.

Mostly I kept my gaze forward, watching the pilot work. But as we approached Rancho Cielo En La Tierra, I did manage to take a look at the scenery.

I loathed it. Remote didn't even begin to describe it.

I always believed Texas was the end of nowhere, but I realized I hadn't seen the end of nowhere until I saw this place. We flew over dry brown terrain for what seemed like days—or maybe that was just my reaction, because I was clutching the airsick bag like it was a life raft.

There was flat dry brown terrain with light green accents. Then there was flat dry brown terrain with dark gray accents. I recognized those. They were some kind of rock. The Texans were calling this terrain mountainous. By Washington State standards, the "mountains" barely rose to the level of "mound."

Finally, the plane crested over one of those rocky areas. A twisty road cut through the brown, and beyond it, I could see buildings.

The ranch.

Thirty-five thousand acres with hunting, fishing, horseback riding, and ATV tours. Lots of historic sites, if you consider ancient burial grounds unlucky enough to be on land that had been private for nearly three centuries to be historical, rather than something that should've been give back to the Native

Americans who had been fighting a court battle for it for the past fifty years.

A lot of rooms, three onsite restaurants (breakfast alone cost nearly five times breakfast at Denny's), and a meeting center in the round building that everything revolved around.

High-thread-count sheets, your own private butler, and the ability to cook in your room if you wanted to spend a minimum of $800 per night. And none of that included fannish staples, like a TV in every room and free wireless.

In fact, if anyone wanted to watch television, they had to do so on a big television in the "game room" (which wasn't a fannish game room by any stretch) because that big TV was the only one attached to the satellite dish.

Whoever thought this place would make for a good sf convention had to have been smoking something. Or really really wanted to keep the riffraff out.

We landed on an airstrip far enough from the main compound that someone had to meet us with a limousine. The limo was stocked with Cristal and caviar and all manner of other goodies.

The complexities of getting to the site were beginning to bother me, although I kept trying to remind myself how stressed and unhappy I would feel if I had driven a Texas interstate to get here.

Twenty minutes later, the limo pulled into a gated area and around an ostentatious water fountain made of red adobe that matched the buildings along either side of us.

I didn't see any fen, which was unusual, given that this was an sf convention. And then I saw some of my people, coming out of one of the long adobe buildings and stopping when they saw our limo.

I didn't recognize any of them, but two were elaborately dressed as elves from Tolkien, and one of those elves held a baby who was wearing a long white-blond wig à la Orlando Bloom's Legolas. (I said I recognized my people; I didn't say we were always brilliant.)

Our limo took us to a building at the end of the winding driveway. "Your rooms are here, gentlemen," the limo driver said. "May I carry your bags?"

Since he knew where we were going, and we didn't, we decided to let him carry *my* bags. I had brought all of my clothing, and some high-end laptops, including two that were brand new and waiting for Spade-designed software, in case I needed a clean machine.

Dave and Groot hadn't brought any luggage at all. Groot planned to buy what he needed at the con, apparently forgetting we were so far away from the Real World that buying socks and underwear would be impossible, and Dave said he would borrow from another SMoF, an image I still couldn't quite erase from my mind.

The limo driver carried my bags to a room at the end of one of the long adobe buildings. While we walked, I called Paladin.

"When are you getting here?" she demanded.

"I'm here," I said. "Where do you need me?"

"Jerkwad's suite. I'll text the coordinates," she said and hung up.

In spite of myself, I smiled. Every now and then, she sounded just like the sf fan hidden beneath that tough exterior.

The text arrived seconds later. Not only had she sent me the location, but she had actually sent me an interactive map. It asked for a push notification, wanting my location, which I did not grant. I don't let anyone into my phone for any reason.

Instead, I showed the map to the limo driver and he showed me the shortest route to get there. In fact, he offered to drive me.

We put my bags inside my room. The only part of it that registered was its size. I took thirty seconds to put on a new T-shirt, because I had sweated through the last one. I couldn't face Paladin layered in sweat.

Then I had the limo driver take me to Jerkwad's suite.

Although "suite" was the wrong word. So was "cabin." It was a bungalow, with an entrance made of tiles that were, I realized, of the Texas state flag. Red, white, and dark blue flowers bloomed alongside the door, and as I walked toward it, I realized the white flowers bloomed in the shape of a star.

That was excessive, but it seemed like everything here was.

Paladin stood before the door, arms crossed. She's maybe 5'4" on a good day, with elfin features and actual god-given pointed ears, but she carries herself like she could take on everyone in Mordor by herself and still have some fight left over.

She wore a white tank T-shirt with an image of two famous female anime characters exchanging a lurid kiss emblazoned across the front. I was sure that was no accident.

She completed the outfit with deliberately distressed jeans and shitkickers so kickery that they should have had hobnails along the front.

"Took long enough," she said. "I needed you here yesterday."

I didn't remind her that she had only called me two hours before.

"He's been dead that long?" I asked.

"*No,*" she said. Then pursed her lips. "I don't know. None of us do. He arrived, had some lunch with the concom, and retired to his room. They found him when he didn't show up for some breakfast panel that he had asked them to schedule. I don't know all the details."

"If they think this is murder, why are there no cops here?" I asked.

"Do you know where you are, Spade?" She jangled some keys

at me. Behind me, the limo purred to a start and drove off.

"Um...Texas?" I said, because she wanted me to answer her. It was hot out here, and smelled of dust and rotted vegetation. I assumed that was the "perfume" of the flowers.

"No," she said firmly. "We are in the Republic of Texas, where Santa Ana lost, and Davy Crockett lived, and somehow the Great God Sam Houston managed to save them all."

She reached forward and unlocked the door. I felt cool air-conditioned air.

"What did you do?" I asked, not quite willing to go in there yet.

"I told them that they *had* to call the authorities, and they said they already had, and they were going to declare him dead from a distance, and ship him home to his family—if he has family."

Her lips thinned, and on her cheeks two dots of red appeared, which was a tame version of the angry look she had apparently shared with the concom as she was talking to them.

"I told them they couldn't Scalia this thing." By that, she meant they couldn't have a justice of the peace, who acted as a coroner in the rural parts of Texas, declare the death natural causes without even viewing the body. That had happened when Supreme Court Justice Antonin Scalia died in Texas in early 2016 at a ranch further south from here.

Unlike Scalia, who had been 79 and in poor health, Jerkwad was maybe 35, and just fine, as far as I knew. I would have wagered that Jerkwad probably hadn't seen his doctor twice in the past week, like Scalia had just before his death.

"They told me," Paladin was saying, "that under Texas law, they could do whatever they wanted, and I told them we were not going to have conspiracy theories mar science fiction conventions forever—"

Like conspiracy theories had marred the death of Scalia.

"—and if they wanted to go through me to get to the body, they were welcome to do so, but if they didn't, then they'd better get the hell out of my way."

She gave me a feral little grin.

"It's good to have a fierce reputation," she said. "They've left me alone so far."

I nodded, my heart pounding. I didn't like this.

"*Someone's* going to investigate this, right?" I asked. "I'm not qualified to judge dead bodies."

"Someone will," she said. "I called everyone I could think of. I told them that there was a serious crisis here and we needed a real medical examiner. I threatened, I pulled strings, and long story short, we're getting a qualified medical examiner from Lubbock. I expected him here before you. Now I have to call again, and see what the hold-up is."

"But no police," I said.

"Texas State Police sent one officer," she said with a frown. "Apparently safe-guarding the body is less important than making sure no one flees the ranch."

"That might be so," I said. "Although they let us in."

"You can check in any time you like," she sang to the tune of "Hotel California," misquoting the song.

I knew the rest. Apparently, I could never leave. Wonderful. This day was just getting better and better.

We stepped inside the room. My first thought was that it was colder than it should have been to determine time of death, but what did I know? I got most of my knowledge of crime scenes from *CSI* and mystery novels.

The room had a sour smell—like a filthy bathroom—but over that was a kind of sweet scent that I thought I recognized, but couldn't identify.

The room actually had a little entryway, and a big kitchen

area, along with a living room. There were two tubs of ice cream melting in the sink, the scoop on a dish rack, no bowls.

I frowned at that. Paladin didn't even look at it. She stopped at the door to the bedroom and glared at me, as if I should have been following right behind her. I probably should have: we were heading toward the body, after all. If we touched anything on our journey, we were as dumb as the minor characters in any afore-mentioned *CSI* episode.

I reached her side. The sour smell was stronger here. The curtains were closed, but the overhead light was on, the light pale compared to the sunlight creeping across the floor.

The bed had a giant mound on it. A laptop was toppled on its side, open, the screen dark. A pale hand rested near it, as if trying to reach it one last time. A phone was charging on the nightstand, and a tablet was resting on top of that missing bowl, that was probably filled with melted ice cream.

I frowned at that mound on the bed, thinking at first it was a pile of pillows or extra blankets or something. I gingerly walked to the edge of the bed, and realized, as I got closer, that the mound on the bed was Jerkwad.

He was the size of five Jerkwads—at least the Jerkwad from my memory. That scrawny foul-mouthed kid who made fun of me for being fat had become fat himself. Fatter than I am or ever had been.

"Oh, wow," I said, startled to hear my own voice.

Paladin didn't say anything. She just let me look.

Jerkwad was on his back, his fleshy face bloodless, his mouth open slightly, and his eyes staring at nothing. One hand reached toward the laptop, the other rested on his amazingly large stomach. The blankets were pulled up to his armpits, and the pillows—all of them—were either under his head or supporting his back.

"Last time I saw him," I said quietly, "he weighed maybe 100 pounds soaking wet."

"And who in the name of Sweet Jesus are you?" demanded a deep baritone voice.

I started, looking at the body as if it had spoken to me. My heart was hammering.

"Who the hell are *you?*" Paladin asked.

"Nathan Reyes, from the medical examiner's office. Who the hell are *you?*"

A short man was standing just behind her, wearing a black cowboy hat, black shirt, jeans, and boots that looked custom-made.

"I'm the person that called and demanded you get here," Paladin said.

I stepped forward before she alienated him completely. I stuck out my hand, gave him my legal name, and said, "Thank you for coming."

He looked at me. Fortunately, the new T-shirt I had put on wasn't one of my offensive ones. It was dark blue with a tiny almost invisible logo from a long-defunct D.C. convention.

"What're you people doing here?" he snapped, not taking my hand.

"Waiting for you," Paladin said in the same tone.

I held up a hand. "We're the closest thing the convention has to people with real-world law enforcement experience, who aren't lawyers. We figured you didn't want any of the lawyers here."

"I don't want any of you here," he said. "But I will photograph you where you're standing, if you don't mind."

Paladin opened her mouth as if she was going to object, but I said, "We don't mind," before she could speak.

He removed an older digital camera with a lot of extras—telephoto lens, special flash, and some things I didn't recognize—and nearly blinded me as he took a few shots.

"Now, get out and let me do my job," he said. "Give your names again to my assistant on your way out."

I nodded, grabbed Paladin's arm, and led her out of the room. She looked over her shoulder, struggling ever so slightly. I couldn't tell if she wanted to give him a piece of her mind or if she wanted to share something important.

Not that it mattered, because I wasn't going to let her talk to him at all anymore. Not as long as the murder rumors were flying.

We hurried through the living area, Paladin shaking off my hand as we went. She pulled open the door as a stocky woman, dressed just like Reyes, entered, carrying two bags.

"We're supposed to give you our names," I said, before Paladin slipped away.

"One minute," she said.

We stepped back into the heat, and the sweat that had dried on me revitalized, drenching this shirt. Great. Another thing to love about Texas.

Paladin shifted from one foot to the other. She didn't want to wait but she was smart enough to know that if we left now, we would look suspicious.

The assistant returned, grabbed a notepad from her back pocket, and said, "O.K. Shoot." which I thought to be a remarkably poor choice of words.

I gave her my name, and the business card I used when I was going to court.

Paladin looked at me pointedly. "I'll meet you in the lobby of the convention," she said.

She still didn't want me to know her real name.

I nodded, and walked away, feeling a little deflated. Paladin protected her privacy more than any other person I had ever met. I respected it. I just wished she included me inside the network of people she trusted with her name—if there were any.

I had no idea where the lobby was. I had to find the resort's map on my phone, which had some coverage here, surprising me, until I remembered that heads of state had visited this ranch. I walked in the blazing sun, past the ridiculous fountain, which didn't even manage to splash me (dammit) to a roundish adobe building that looked—from the outside at least—larger than the others.

It had two large entry doors underneath an overhang with a border done in the same Lone Star Flag tiles as the ones outside Jerkwad's room. I shoved my phone into the carrier I kept for it on my belt, pushed open the double doors—

And hit a cacophony of shouting voices. The sound was so loud that it actually made me take a step backward. It didn't help that the lobby itself was all tile and plain walls, with a vaulted ceiling that sparkled as if it had somehow captured the stars.

The shouters were all to my right, clustered near the front desk. Behind the desk, a harried-looking dark-haired woman cradled a phone between her ear and shoulder, while holding a cell phone to the other ear. The woman beside her, also harried-looking but with ash blonde hair so uniform that it could only have come from a bottle, determinedly pounded a keyboard, while a third woman—clearly a science fiction fan from her build and her Deadpool "I love Chimichangas" T-shirt—watched all of it.

It took me a moment to realize the Chimichanga woman was Millie. I hadn't seen her in nearly a year. Half of her hair had gone gray, and she had put on weight.

I went around the screamers, hearing only parts of the argument. Along with the standard "It's all your fault" found in any argument, I was also treated to "Well, you invited him" and "I had nothing to do with the money" and "Are you saying *I* took it?"

I was a little surprised at the composition of the screamers. They were a mixed bunch. A third of them were the ones who had been desperately trying to placate everyone at the Worldcon a few years back, the Worldcon that had replicated only the very first Worldcon in 1939 for the depth of the hatreds that had come out of it. The rest were a mixture of the we-need-diversity crowd (who, not coincidentally, happened to be diverse) and the white bigots who had opposed them.

I recognized six out of the twelve screamers: Two female graduates of the Clarion Writers Workshop who had published a few stories and received enough award nominations to take themselves a bit too seriously were screaming at three male hard science fiction writers (who had as many award nominations and two more wins than the Clarion group). A female urban fantasy writer who published her own works and made more money than all the screamers put together was trying to calm them down.

At that moment, I realized I was looking at the idiots who had thought they could run a convention better than any fan-run convention, because they had writing credentials, awards, and Good Intentions.

If only Paladin hadn't called me. If only Millie had. I didn't have an inappropriate crush on Millie. I didn't have *any* crush on Millie. I could have said no, had some marvelous Texas Barbecue with friends in Garland, and been none the wiser.

I made it to Millie's side. She looked over at me and for a minute, I thought she was going to spit in my face.

"I needed you here months ago," she snapped.

What was it with everyone today? Had hello gone out the window in favor of telling Spade he was needed and late?

"You needed to shut this down months ago," I said, looking around. Through the half-open door behind the front desk, I saw two men in suits, also on the phone, talking to another writer I sort-of recognized. I knew he was one of the young enthusiastic we-don't-need-no-stinkin-fans folks, but I had no idea which camp of screamers he belonged in.

"I can't get you a room," Millie said.

I let out a snort, that got drowned out by a shout of "I did *not* mismanage anything!" coming from the screamers.

"I have a room," I said. "My bags are already in it."

"Sorry," Millie said flatly. "I should have been more precise. I cannot pay for your room."

I looked around the lobby. There were screaming writers, no fans except for Millie, a dead Nazi-wannabe several doors down, and heat so potent outside that it made me want to fall over just thinking about it.

I had nothing to stay for. The dead asshole was being handled by the authorities, and I didn't want to get involved in whatever this was.

"Fine," I said. "I haven't really used it yet, so I'll be on my way."

Millie grabbed my hand in both of hers, and leaned into me. "You were a Microsoft Millionaire, right?" she asked. "I heard that you're worth a fortune. Is that true?"

I was and am a Microsoft Millionaire. Unlike most of my colleagues, I didn't spend my millions when I left Microsoft. I had invested them. Wisely.

But I never talked about my finances. To anyone. Ever.

I extricated my hand from hers. "I can afford the room, Millie. I just see no reason to stay here."

Behind me, the screamers erupted in "I gave the checks to you!" and "You were handling the credit cards, not me!"

I nearly closed my eyes. I was beginning to understand what was going on here, and I needed to get out before I became the only person who could solve it.

"All of our Big Name Pros bailed on us," Millie said.

"After you sent half of them a form letter, reneging on your initial promise of a thousand-dollar appearance fee plus expenses." I had watched that one from afar, and wondered why Millie had stayed attached to the convention.

"I'm so sorry, Miss Dash," said the ash blonde woman to Millie. "I'm being told I can't negotiate with you because you are not on our list of organizers."

"Oh, for crumb's sake," Millie said to the woman. "Just give me a minute, okay?"

She grabbed my arm and moved me closer to the screamers, as if that would enable me to hear her better.

"Spade," she said, leaning as close to me as she could, "we need to pay the hotel $250,000 to hold us for the next three days. Can you help?"

I felt my mouth drop open. Who knew that was a true involuntary reaction and not just something characters did in books?

"Um, just delay," I said. "You have a deposit, right?"

"And we gave them a check yesterday for the rest of it, like we were supposed to do according to our contract," she said. "The check bounced."

"What?" I had heard of this happening at cons in the past, but I had never seen it. And at a high-end resort. Usually, the con fees were less than $100,000 at this point in the proceedings.

"The check bounced," she said, "and that's not the worst thing. Any money we put into the account, like the credit card fees for same-day registration, that money vanishes too."

I frowned. Someone was tampering with the con's bank account.

"Not," she said, "that there were many same-day registrations. Only three people showed up today. Right now, it looks like we'll have maybe 300 con-goers and all of our guests."

"All of your remaining guests," I said.

"We planned for fifteen hundred," she said. "We *budgeted* for fifteen hundred."

"You know better than this, Millie," I said, because I couldn't help myself. "Why are you even involved?"

The screamers escalated. They had devolved into that very adult argument: "Did not!" "Did too!" "Did not!" "Did too!"

Millie had to lean closer. She smelled faintly of onions.

"I like them," she said, nodding toward the screaming concom. "Or I did. I always planned the Clarion parties, and I got to know everyone else at some local conventions, and they're *nice people*, Spade."

"Well, fuck you too," one of the screamers shouted. "I've had enough of this!"

He started to walk off, when another screamer grabbed his arm. "We're all liable, asshole. Someone didn't get us nonprofit status."

"What?" the screamers asked in unison.

The arm-grabber looked at all of them. "We had a meeting," he said. "We discussed this. We're all personally liable for every expense."

I leaned close to Millie. "And that," I said, "is why I'm not helping you."

"Spade, please," she said. "There's something—"

"Hey!" Someone touched my back. I turned and found myself face to crew-cut with one of the non-Clarion concom people. His skin was red with anger and sunburn. "You're...Ellery Queen, right?"

I didn't answer him. But to be fair, I couldn't, for the life of me, remember his name either.

Millie said, "He's Spade. We call him Spade."

Crew-cut ignored her. "And you solve crimes, right?"

I still didn't answer him. I did not want to get involved.

"Leave him alone, Jack," Millie said.

Then his name came to me. Jack Burwell, three-time Nebula nominee, two-time Hugo nominee, sore loser, and one of the architects of all the nightmarish in-fighting. I remembered him now, and I wanted nothing to do with him.

"Excuse me," I said, and pushed past him.

The screamers had stopped yelling, all of them watching me now. Paladin hadn't arrived yet. Maybe I could head her off, because at the moment, I would pay the limo driver that full $250,000 to get me the hell out of here.

"Spade, please," Millie said. "Jack's right. You could figure out what happened to the money."

I stopped and closed my eyes. I probably *could* figure it out. That didn't mean I wanted to.

"Not here, you can't," said a male voice.

I couldn't help myself. I pivoted one more time.

One of the men from the back room had come out to the front desk. "You all will vacate the premises immediately, and you will hear from our attorneys forthwith."

Forthwith? Who said forthwith? And then I realized he had a British accent. He had been brought in to run this place from somewhere far, far, far from West Texas.

And he was serious.

I did not reach for my credit card. Instead, I nodded at him, to let him know I understood. Then I headed for the door—only to see Groot come forward with a black American Express card in his hot little hand.

"You take AmEx, right?" he asked the man at the desk. "I'll cover this."

The concom was watching Groot in surprise. At that moment, I realized none of them knew that he was one of the most famous fen in the history of fandom.

No wonder this thing had failed.

"They won't be able to pay you back, Groot," I said.

"Oh, they will," he said. "Because, before I pay this, they're going to all sign promissory notes to me."

He gave me an evil grin. The one thing I had learned about Groot on the car ride to the airport was how much he hated the infighting that had been going on in science fiction lately, and how much he blamed both groups of "professional" writers for it.

He also told me that as a gay man who had been a longtime member of fandom, he had never been bullied until the last few years—and some of the bullying was because the online behavior of some of the people attending this convention seemed to give the socially inept permission to use hate speech at conventions themselves.

These idiots running this concom no idea who Groot was or how happily he would screw them if they stiffed him. In fact, I believed he *wanted* to screw them, which was why he made this offer. I finally understood why Groot had got us that plane.

Unlike the concom, though, Millie knew who he was, and she probably guessed why he was offering to save the convention.

She clutched at my arm. "Oh, my god, Spade, please, please, for the sake of our community, please help us find that money."

If she had repeated her request for me to pay for the convention, I would have said no. But this...this intrigued me. I had no idea how money could disappear in such a way to make the concom scream at each other in public on the first day of the convention.

Besides, when a bondage group commandeered an East Coast convention, and broke the sprinkler system, ruining the entire hotel, fandom paid for that for years. We were banned from that hotel chain, even though we had nothing to do with the people who ruined the hotel. They hadn't even registered at the convention.

This time, our people—or a subset of our people—had set up this convention at this ridiculously expensive and out-of-the-way ranch, where only the most powerful go, and failing to resolve this could have reverberations in fandom—and politically—for more than a decade.

I sighed.

"Let me see the books," I said to her.

"He doesn't get to see the books," said one of the Nebula women. "We need a certified public account—"

"Shut the fuck up, LaToya," Jack Burwell said.

The woman—whose name I couldn't remember either, but which I knew wasn't LaToya—turned purple with rage. Burwell had done that on purpose, comparing a Black woman to one of the lesser Jacksons, as if the Jacksons were the only Blacks he knew.

"My name, you *asshole*, is Leslie," she said. "And I can't believe you don't remember it. You're such a *pig*."

"There are actually guns here that you can rent," Millie said so that only I could hear. "And I'm thinking of renting a few."

"Ellery Queen here," Burwell said, "is some kind of financial wizard, aren't you, Queen?"

He put an emphasis on the word *Queen*, and I finally figured out why he had chosen that moniker for me. He was using it as an epithet.

Groot had been leaning on the front desk, but he turned around, his eyes glittering with fury.

"You, Burwell," Groot said, "get your friends and come with me. We'll do the documentation first, before I pay for this. I just had to reassure the hotel that I would."

"We can't do documentation without a lawyer," Burwell

snapped.

"Lucky for you, I am one." Groot's gaze met mine. The fury hadn't abated, but it was now evident only in the tightness around his jaw. "Let's go."

"I won't sign anything," Burwell said.

"Fine," Groot said. "I won't cover your screwup then."

"This Queen guy—"

"His name is *Spade*," Groot said.

"Whatever," Burwell said. "He'll find the money."

"Most likely, you were hacked," I said, "and you'll never get the money back."

"Obi-Wan-Kenobi, he is our only hope," said another one of the crew-cut brigade, who apparently didn't quite realize how serious this all was. Or maybe that was an inept attempt at humor.

"We can't pay you," Burwell said to me.

"Oh, you'll pay me," I said. What I didn't add was that he would pay me at double my usual rate for *mundanes*. I usually charged conventions nothing, and my sf friends a very small rate for forensic accounting. But he wasn't one of my sf friends. Nor was he a friend of sf.

Once again, he was on the verge of destroying the community I loved. So I would step in. Not for Millie. Not for Groot.

For the future. And with the hope that I could find something to keep this convention from reverberating through the fannish community like a financial plague.

———

Operations wasn't even in the same building as the main part of the convention. Ops was four buildings down, on a small rise with a clear view of the brown Texas landscape. At first, I thought that was stupid (especially since it meant I had to walk more in the damn heat), and then I learned that Ops was in the building that housed the business center, and was the only place in the entire ranch that actually had a wireless connection. (Not even the front desk was on wireless. It was *wired*.)

As I walked with Millie, we both noted a white van parked next to the coroner's van. The white van had a blue logo with a yellow star in the center on each side. There were words trailing down one side, but I couldn't read them.

"What's that?" I asked, nodding toward new van.

"Crime Lab techs," she said. "Probably from Lubbock."

Paladin hovered near the building, arms crossed. A few people I didn't recognize—clearly mundanes—were talking to her. She looked up and saw me.

Thinking maybe she was in trouble for staying with the body, I mouthed, *Do you need help?*

She shook her head ever so slightly.

I pointed at her, then I made a replica of a phone with my thumb and little finger, and put it to my ear, and mouthed *If you need me.*

She inclined her head once, and turned away.

Millie and I continued. I needed a beverage. I had sweated through this T-shirt now. On the way to Ops, we stopped and grabbed one of my clean laptops. I didn't even bother with another shirt. Ops was supposed to smell like someone died in it. I'd just help the stench along.

The building was dark when we entered. Ops was locked tight, just like the business center next door. Millie opened the door with a card key, and the lights came on automatically, revealing two small computers, several uncomfortable chairs, and not a single human being.

I had never seen an empty Ops on day one of a convention.

"Where's the security team?" I asked Millie.

"Ha ha ha," she said flatly, meaning there was no security team.

"Jesus, Millie," I said. I'd never heard of a modern sf convention without security. "The liability issues—"

"I'm not official here," she said. "My legal name isn't connected to the convention at all. I just thought I could help."

I hoped that would be enough. This thing was getting worse by the second. "Where's the financial stuff?"

She leaned over one keyboard, tapped the space bar, and a spreadsheet opened. From my position beside her, I could see names, credit card numbers, addresses, and more.

"You're kidding me, right?" I asked. "Tell me someone just accidentally left this open. Tell me it was at least password protected."

She stood up and crossed her arms. "If it was password protected, then everyone would have to know the password, so what's the point?"

From her tone, I could tell she was quoting someone—someone she thought was dumber than rocks.

"No encryption at all?" I asked, feeling breathless. I was a little dizzy and I hoped it was the news, not dehydration and the stress.

"None," she said.

I pulled over one of the inadequate chairs and almost fell into it. It almost fell to the ground.

"I need water, beverages, snacks, and some thumb drives," I said. I wished I could order up a better chair.

"We don't have the money to—"

"You want me to do this?" I asked, sounding more testy than I had in years. "Because I'm going to keel over if I don't get hydrated. I don't care who pays for it. I need water, I need food, and I need it all now."

"Yes, sir," she said. She set the key card next to me, propped the door open, and left.

I scooted the chair to the computer that was sharing all its personal data with the world. Unencrypted on a wireless network, not even a password. These people—

She returned with some cold water that had clearly come from a vending machine. "I called for room service and put it on my tab," she said. "I ordered everything I could think of."

"Thank you," I said, and proceeded to get lost in the digital footprint in front of me.

I had it solved before the food arrived, and the food arrived fast. Pizza, nachos, barbeque—my stomach growled and I filled it, staring at the screen in complete disbelief. I guess the Unity Con folks were asking for this problem, although I wasn't entirely sure why.

Millie was sitting next to me. She was working on her own plate of nachos. "Well?"

"I need you to leave," I said.

"What?" she asked. "I didn't do this. Spade, you know that. I don't know anything about finances."

"Yeah, I know," I said, "but if you don't leave, you're going to spend more time with law enforcement than you want to."

"Oh," she said, and stood up. "You'll give me back the key card."

"Sure," I lied. I ate another piece of pizza as I watched her gather her nacho plate, and a bottle of water. Then she left.

I had to stand too and make sure she wasn't in the hallway. I wasn't dizzy anymore. The cool air had helped, the water had helped, and so had the salty food. Even if the con couldn't pay for my room, I would need it just for the shower alone.

The hallway was empty. I went back into Ops, pushed the door closed, and called Paladin.

She answered, talking, "Spade, I thought I was clear—"

"I need investigators in Ops right now," I said. "Preferably someone who has some bit of computer savvy. Tell them to bag Jerkwad's laptop and keep it away from anyone connected with the convention."

"They already did that," Paladin said. "What did you find?"

"Just send them here, Paladin," I said. I didn't know when she had arrived at the con, and I didn't want her to get in trouble. So I hung up.

And ate. That's what I do when I'm nervous. I eat. So I ate my way through some more pizza, and some wings in the ten minutes it took Paladin and some tall brunette in a crisp blue T-shirt and jeans to get here.

"This is Maria Vega-Hidalgo," Paladin said. "She's the detective on the case. I requested her. We worked together before—on a non-science-fiction case."

Since Paladin often located missing children, I suspected that was the kind of case she was referring to. And I suspected it had been successful, since Vega-Hidalgo didn't seem like someone who would show up willy-nilly at a suspicious death for just anyone.

"I looked up your credentials," Vega-Hidalgo said to me. "You're quite the expert."

She actually sounded impressed, which relieved me.

"What did you find?" Paladin asked.

"First," I said to them both, "tell me why the crime scene people are here."

Paladin looked at Vega-Hidalgo.

Vega-Hidalgo nodded, and said, "We found two empty bottles of insulin and two used syringes beside the bed. The bottles belonged to Mr. Johnson—"

"He was diabetic?" I asked.

"It would seem that way," Vega-Hidalgo said flatly. "There is evidence that he gave himself stomach injections twice daily per doctor's orders. But it looks like he or someone gave him both bottles last night. He was dead by midnight."

I processed that piece of information. Then I swung the computer toward her.

"How much do you know about computers?" I asked. "I don't want to talk down to you."

"Talk to me as if we were in court," she said.

Paladin crossed her arms and leaned against the wall.

Vega-Hidalgo sat down beside me, and I explained what happened, as succinctly as I could.

———

The trail went like this:

Jerkwad boosted the wireless connection at the ranch sometime yesterday, so he could get it in his room. About 10 p.m. last night, he inserted a program into the concom's financial system that would drain the bank accounts and send any money in the accounts—from the time it activated until they got shut down (and they hadn't yet)—to an offshore account in the Cayman Islands.

"Your forensic accountants can track it easily," I said. "Just put $5 in the account and watch it move."

"Then why did it take you so long to figure out?" Paladin asked.

Vega-Hidalgo gave her a sideways glance. From Vega-Hidalgo's perspective, it hadn't taken me long at all.

"Because I wanted to look at Jerkwad's internet trail. I'd love to look in his laptop, but I don't want to mess with it," I said.

"What did you find?" Paladin asked. She knew me too well.

"That Jerkwad is the one who suggested the ranch. He read up on Justice Scalia's death, since it was international news, followed the conspiracy theories, and understood your particular brand of rural justice." I said that last to Vega-Hidalgo. "The coroner system."

"Just because it exists doesn't mean we like it," she said quietly.

"I know," I said. "Jerkwad didn't count on Paladin calling you all. He was counting on his death being ruled natural causes. No one would find where the money went, there would be conspiracy theories, and sf would be hurt for decades to come because of the problems with the hotel."

"He committed suicide?" Paladin asked. "He didn't seem like the type."

"He is exactly the type," I said. "His search history, which I got legitimately, showed a lot of searches for some kind of organ failure due to diabetes in combination with some other disease I've never heard of. I think he was dying, and he wanted to go out with a nasty bang."

"Speculation," Vega-Hidalgo said.

"Yep," I said. "And now, thanks to Paladin, you folks can find the truth."

"I don't get it," Paladin said. "Why don't you think someone from the concom caught him messing with the computers and killed him?"

My turn to raise my eyebrows.

"Really?" I swept my hand toward the computer. "*These* people caught him?"

Paladin shrugged.

"It's a good question," Vega-Hidalgo said.

Paladin smiled slightly. At that moment, I realized she had

asked the question that Vega-Hidalgo hadn't planned on asking but was thinking.

So I answered it straight, without sarcasm.

"I know he did it all because of time of death," I said. "If your people confirm his time of death as sometime before midnight, then the concom didn't do this."

"Because...?" Vega-Hidalgo asked.

"Because the program didn't activate until 3 a.m. The money was in the accounts last night. It was gone by 7 a.m. this morning. If someone on the concom was going to kill him, they would have done so today, not last night."

And, I thought, remembering Millie's comment from earlier, they would have used a gun.

"Speculation," Vega-Hidalgo said again. But her tone was different. This was speculation she understood. "We will have to shut this all down. We'll need to interview everyone, and we'll need to be able to replicate your work, Spade."

I appreciated that she used my con name instead of my real name. She *had* worked with Paladin.

I handed her my clean laptop. "I did the searches on this laptop," I said. "And I have never used it for anything else. It's my gift to your department."

"We'll take it as evidence," she said in a flat, humorlessness Tommy-Lee-Jones-in-*The-Fugitive* voice. "And we'll still need you to talk to our people."

"I'm happy to," I said. "Can we do it in, say, a city? Not here?"

"A city?" Vega-Hidalgo asked. "There's no reason to go to Dallas or Houston."

"I'm sure Lubbock will be fine," Paladin said softly, being the diplomatic one for once.

"That's what I meant," I said. "I just hate this middle-of-nowhere crap."

For the first time since she came into the room, Vega-Hidalgo smiled. "Yes," she said. "We may talk to you in a city. We may even treat you to real Texas food, and even better Texas beer."

"Now we're talking," I said, and smiled.

Maybe this trip wouldn't be a disaster after all.

———

And it wasn't a disaster for me. I got a great hotel room—in Lubbock, thank you very much—excellent food, even better Texas beer, and some wonderful conversations.

We later discovered that Jerkwad had indeed plotted against the idiots running the convention. He had helped them fund the initial deposit, and got a lot of his friends to make reservations, which they later canceled, that led the concom to believe they would have at least 1,500 in attendance.

The concom screwed up the rest. Judging from the programs on Jerkwad's laptop, he had expected encryption just like I had. He must have been very pleased to discover there was none at all. It had made his job much easier.

And he was dying of some strange disease, exacerbated by his heart problems, his diabetes, and his high blood pressure. All of this in a guy 35 years old. Made me want to redouble my efforts at exercise and watching my non-convention eating habits.

He knew he was checking out. So he just picked the time and place for maximum mayhem.

The lawsuits between Groot and the concom continue. I don't pay a lot of attention. I do know that Groot initially planned to forgive the debt of the writers he liked, but by the end of the first few meetings, he decided he didn't like any of them.

Turned out, he said, that some of the people "on his side" were as offensive and bigoted in their attitudes toward the military and sf fans who didn't look like them as the people "on the other side."

He's thinking of punishing them all.

I can't watch. I couldn't watch when this fight originally erupted in sf, and I can't watch now. I'm not a revenge kinda guy.

I like my sf cons to be havens where everyone gets along—or at least tries to. I hate the bullying and nastiness that's moved from the fringes to the center of the community. In the past, we used to look away from some of this stuff. Which meant we tolerated too much bad behavior—and that's changing. But it also meant we had friends from all over every spectrum you could think of. Inept, socially awkward friends, friends we disagreed with. But friends.

I'm working to make that return. Without using some kind of stupid moniker like Unity Con, but instead by acknowledging all parts of our community. We've learned some things in the past few years. We need better grievance committees. We need to make sure we make everyone in our communities comfortable. And we need to put a lid on the bullying.

We're trying.

But I have to admit: I'm glad Jerkwad's gone. And I'm happy that we caught him before he did permanent damage.

And I hope that the next Jerkwad who rises to the fore—and there will be one; there always is—isn't as smart or as psychopathic as this one was.

We dodged a bullet quite literally, and I can't take any credit for it.

All the credit goes to Paladin, stubbornly standing in front of Jerkwad's room in the hot Texas sun, and not letting anyone near him.

Paladin, who loves this community as much as I do.

Even if she'll never say so out loud.

AT WITT'S END

A SPADE/PALADIN CONUNDRUM

Brendan Witt died at age 62 in August of that year. Terrible year. An election year like no other, with both candidates screaming insults at each other, things so beyond the pale that teachers didn't want to have their students watch the news and learn about the election.

As the fall progressed, and my friends—both left and right—began decrying the state of the horrid election, and my religious friends began to ask where God had gone in all of this, I ended up with a pat fannish answer.

God's busy, I'd say. *He's backing up St. Peter at the Pearly Gates, because Witt is standing outside, arguing in his indomitable way that he had to return to his life to get at least ten years of Social Security, so that he could reap what he had sown.*

People laughed as I said that, because they had known Witt. Most of them had been on the other side of his arguments.

Witt and I were two of many fen (hard-core science fiction fans) known by only one name. Witt because it suited him, and me because I had become the go-to guy for crime solving. Since the mid-1990s, I've solved everything at conventions from minor hoaxes to kidnappings.

Witt's death wasn't a crime, even though it was sad. He died just before the start of the Dead Dog party at the World Science Fiction convention. He had been alone in his hotel room, about to take a shower from the looks of it, and he had just keeled over. Later, the coroner said he died of complications of diabetes.

I had been at the convention so I'd been the one to handle all the concerns with the body. I tried not to think about the implications of Witt's death, but it was hard not to. His death was the second time that year that I'd seen a dead body connected to diabetes.

Miraculously, I haven't contracted diabetes yet, although my doc said I would eventually if I kept up my habits. I'm six-six and more than 400 pounds. I've been trying to add in exercise, which feels ridiculous at my size, and I'm thinking of eating better. Eating better means learning how to be a different person, and I'm not sure I'm up to the challenge.

Besides, I've been busy. (I'm always busy.) Witt had left his entire estate to a major Northwest charity and had asked that the money get funneled through the fannish organization that ran one of the major Northwest science fiction conventions. Witt had put that in his will so that the convention would hold a charity auction to raise matching funds to his "donation." But what his convoluted inheritance actually became was an excuse for me to take control of the estate and make sure it had gotten taken care of smoothly.

Witt's estate was worth upwards of two million dollars at today's prices. I didn't have all of the cash yet, because I was figuring out how to sell most of his prize collectables, but I valued them at only one-quarter of their worth, due to the vagaries of the market.

Still, the two million was causing me issues. Even though Witt wanted the auction to be held in the Northwest, no con was big enough to have a matching-funds auction that would bring in two million dollars. I didn't want to be spending the rest of my life holding charity auctions to match funds to Witt's estate, so I toyed with holding the auction at Comic-Con.

But Comic-Con had moved out of the fannish realm and into the Event realm. The fen started complaining about the venue choice. To make matters worse, the fen made it clear they wanted to hold several fannish funerals, held at each convention that Witt attended regularly.

Witt had expressly told me (and others) hundreds of times how he loathed fannish funereal tradition. He thought fannish funerals morbid. He also thought them silly, because usually, the people eulogizing the deceased had only met that person a few times. I'd remind people that Witt said these things, and no one seemed to care. The fannish organization, which usually deferred to me on all things Witt, didn't defer this time. The fen wanted to send Witt off in style, and it didn't matter to them that the style was one he would have hated.

If I wanted to carry out Witt's matching fund wishes, then the only thing I could do was set up the world's most kickass charity auction and give it double-billing with Witt's one and *only* fannish memorial service.

I decided to hold the charity auction at the biggest West Coast science fiction convention held in that year.

The Left Coast BigCon used to be called the Megacon back in the day, but the name had been usurped by one of those corporate comic/gaming companies. The problem with the new name was BigCon wasn't really big at all, not compared with the way all of the comic conventions had grown recently. But the BigCon was the biggest sf con we had to offer on the West Coast—and I didn't dare move east. That would have been a bridge too far for the fen.

I made the auction itself an event. I pulled out all the stops, and guilted dozens of writers, artists, and old-time collector friends of Witt to donate thousands of items to the auction. Then I advertised the auction separately from, and in tandem with, the convention. I wanted big name collectors to show up, even if they weren't from the West Coast.

I billed the auction *The Wittiest, Foulest, Most Entertaining Charity Auction in the Entire Universe! Join Us To Get Your Paws on Great and Rare Things!*

And I added this in smaller font:

Memorialize our friend Witt by doing what he loved best— handling collectibles, raising money, and helping others. (His other favorite pastime, arguing for arguing's sake, will be allowed, but only outside the room.)

I figured most people would be stunned at the "helping others" phrase, because Witt kept his generosity secret. I also thought most people would laugh knowingly at the arguing part. I wanted that arguing part so that people would actually show up for Witt, not just for the collectibles.

But I was worried about attendance. That was why I let rumors start that newly located items from the estates of some of sf's great collectors—Forrest J. Ackerman's mythic Hollywood memorabilia, and Bill Trojan's spectacular book collection. We actually didn't have any of that stuff. Forry had sold off most of his collection before he died, and a lot of Trojan's collection had been sold intact to private collectors.

I expected collectors to appear because they were mercenary.

What I hadn't expected were all the people who were showing up because they were friends of Witt.

When the chair of BigCon finally approached me, asking what

we were going to do with the auction—and finally got through to me about the fact that we were going to have upwards of a thousand people at the auction—we had to rent the biggest space possible from the hotel. A space big enough to put the stuff on display, and large enough to handle the gigantic crowd of collectors.

It was all last-minute, which I loathed. I'm a planner, and my planning had gone out the window.

Then the convention began, and people started pulling me aside to tell me stories about Witt.

He paid for my family's move to Arizona, said a Big Name Fan, *so I could get a good job, not the crap-ass thing I had in the Midwest.*

He paid my way through rehab, said another.

He gave me enough money to allow me and my children to flee my abusive husband, one timid writer told me.

The stories continued. One sentence here, another sentence there. Mostly whispered at me, because Witt had made each and every person promise they would tell no one.

He didn't want his largess known.

I had thought I was one of Witt's closest friends.

Turned out, I hadn't known him at all.

———

The pre-auction ceremony (read funeral) started without me. I figured staying away from the actual memorial was the least I could do to honor Witt's no-memorial-service rule.

Besides, the entire thing had morphed into a mini-convention of its own. Daniel Deggs, the con's Toastmaster and Raconteur Extraordinaire, who had been tapped as the auction's Master of Ceremonies, had even divided the day into little segments.

The first segment became the memorial service's opening ceremonies, another irony, since Witt *loathed* opening ceremonies. He had told me a thousand times that he would only attend opening ceremonies if someone had convinced him that an attractive woman would run through the room naked.

There were no naked women, but there were belly dancers, a Washington State opening ceremonies tradition. Most of the dancers had—you guessed it—been beneficiaries of Witt's secret charitable impulses. These women wanted to dance in his memory, and dance they did.

I arrived late, but not too late for that. The Pacific Northwest fannish belly dancers were among the best in the world.

The usual suspects were there, including folks from the dealer's room who should have been tending their tables. I nearly tripped over megacollector Dwight William Weeks's wheelchair as I came in, and asked him if he wanted to move closer to the front. He shook his head. He wasn't as big a fan of the belly dancers as I was.

I stood near him in the back, arms crossed, and listened in surprise as person after person broke their oath to Witt.

Deggs started it all by giving them permission to speak.

"After all," Deggs said, as he launched into the memorial part of the memorial, "what did Witt say to all of us about his fate after death?"

What do I care? The room shouted back en masse. *I'll be dead!*

A shiver ran through me. I thought I had known Witt best of all. Had I been wrong? Had he presented that so-called secret self to everyone he helped?

"And since he's dead," Deggs said, proving this was, indeed, a fannish funeral and not the kind of carefully scripted be-nice-to-the-family funeral that happened in the mundane (non-sf) world, "let's talk honestly about Witt."

What a gamble. Because Witt had viciously insulted pretty much everyone in science fiction.

Person after person got up, walked down an incredibly long aisle, and grabbed the microphone from Deggs. Every single person described an epic verbal battle they had had with Witt, why they had thought Witt was an utter asshole back when they met him, and then they'd tell a story of generosity.

Almost every story ended with *And he told me not to tell anyone, because he didn't want his reputation ruined.*

"This would have made him so mad," Dwight muttered.

"Yeah," I said. Witt really had never wanted anyone to praise him. He wasn't that kind of man. Gratitude made him nervous.

But Dwight and I seemed to be the only grumpy souls in the room.

No one looked at the collectibles, which lined the walls. Some of the art glittered, because I had put special lighting near it. Other, more delicate valuable things, sat in shaded areas on the sides, so that light wouldn't destroy them.

I looked at the hundreds of items we had to get through. We were nearly an hour behind schedule, and we had been pushing the timeline from the beginning.

I glanced at Deggs, hoping he felt the time pressure too. The man's face was slightly red, and, as I watched, he surreptitiously raised his right hand, leaned his head toward it, and wiped underneath his right eye with his thumb.

Good heavens, he was crying. Had Witt done him a kindness too?

If so, this Witt love-fest would never end.

My heart was hammering in my chest. I pushed off the wall I'd been leaning on, and walked up the side aisle, past the memorabilia from the first *Star Wars* movie back in 1977, past the collectables from the original *Star Trek* TV series, past the key issues of several Marvel comics, ready for bids. Deggs saw me, and tried to shake me off, but I was channeling Witt.

We only had this room until midnight, and I had done the math. I figured it would take at least eight hours to go through all this stuff, and then there would be the two hours (minimum) we needed for payment and organization. Yeah, we could do some of it on Sunday, but not all of it. We were on the clock.

Then a hand grabbed my arm. I looked down to see Paladin standing next to me. Her eyes were clear, but her eyelashes were spikey as if moisture had stuck them together.

I tried to make that compute. Paladin was here? And she had teared up? Both things, I figured, were next to impossible.

I had known Paladin for years now. She and I had worked cases together, and I'm pretty sure she saved my life once.

Even with all of that, I don't know Paladin's real name. She's managed to keep it from me—rather like Witt kept all of his acts of generosity from me.

"I need to talk to you," Paladin said in a quiet voice.

She looked tired, something I'd never quite seen before. Paladin is small and strong. Sometimes I think she's a pixie or a member of the fae. She's the only person I know in real life (not in fannish makeup) who has real God-given pointed ears.

Normally, I would have done anything Paladin asked, but we were on the clock—

"*Now*," she said, in a not-so-quiet voice.

Then she herded me through a side door that led into the kitchen area, a door I had insisted on keeping locked, so that the collectibles would stay safe. The fact that the door was unlocked caught my attention almost as much as the determination on Paladin's face.

In the fluorescent light, I saw that she was wearing her signature black T-shirt and black jeans. Only, for once, her T-shirt did not have an image or a message. She was wearing black, as in mourning clothes.

As in funeral clothes.

Which meant that she too had known Witt.

How did I not know that?

"This thing is running behind," I said.

"Good," she said, "because we have a problem."

I frowned at her, resisting the urge to glance at the door. "What is it?"

"The fanzines are gone," she said.

The fanzines, mimeographed and mailed to fen all over the world, had kept sf fandom alive in the era before the internet. The fanzines were amateur magazines that sometimes had followings as big as the prozines (the regular magazines).

The collection of fanzines we had at this auction was truly special. We had rare, famous and hard-to-find issues of fanzines that some had believed only existed in fannish lore. We had several issues of *Stymie*, written and published by the late film critic Roger Ebert when he was still a kid in school. We had the first issue of what most believe to be the first fanzine, *Comet*, published in 1930, and signed by both of its creators, Raymond Palmer and Walter Dennis. We had all five issues of *Science Fiction*, the 1933 fanzine edited by Jerry Siegel who (with Joe Shuster) went on to create Superman, which we were selling as a lot.

We had the tenth issue of OSFAN, published in 1970, prized because it marked the first publication of the notorious *Eye of Argon*, written by a sixteen-year-old Jim Theis. The story was well known, not because it was good, but because it was famously bad, and the fen had adopted reading it aloud as a party game.

My favorite donation, though, and the one that had generated the most interest was the legendary thirteenth issue of *Goop, Grope, and Grimm*, published on Halloween, 1963. It contained

"The Adventures of Morgana Jones," the most famous piece of fan fiction ever written. The story predicted Kennedy's assassination less than a month away, at Dallas, in a school bookstore (close enough), as well as the rise of *Star Trek*, which the story had called *Wagon Train in Space*. Coincidentally (or not), that title was how Roddenberry pitched the show to the Hollywood suits.

Arguments in fannish circles debated whether the author, the pseudonymous Walter Waltine Waltette (or W^3 as he became known), was actually psychic or friends with both Lee Harvey Oswald and Gene Roddenberry—which seemed to me to be highly improbable, although not as improbable as the other theories as to why the story was so chockful of future lore. Some believed a time traveler wrote it; others simply claimed the fanzine had the wrong date on the cover and had actually appeared in 1968 not 1963. Other fen claimed they had received their copy in early November 1963, and had been shocked at the ties to the Kennedy assassination.

However, no one in the government had ever investigated W^3, at least as far as we knew, although the House Select Committee on Assassinations talked to a variety of fen in 1977, trying to track down W^3, to see what he knew. Not even the editor/publisher of *Goop, Grope, and Grimm*, Ike Gopnik, knew him. Ike claimed under oath before Congress that the story had shown up on his doorstep in early July 1963, and he thought it cool, so he published it.

Ike had dined out on his moment in the Congressional spotlight for another decade, before he went to the Great Convention in the Sky. However, the issue of *Goop, Grope, and Grimm*, like a lot of other things in this auction, had come from his private collection.

That collection had been rescued—quite literally—from a Dumpster by a Big Name Fan who shall remain nameless for the purposes of this tale. Now that fan was getting up there, and he was divesting himself of the parts of his collection he knew he would never look at again.

The fanzine collection had been the most complete collection I had ever seen. I had heard, from the fannish grapevine, that no one had seen a collection like it. There were gems in those mimeographed sheets that most of us had believed to be creations of fannish lore, not actual fanzines themselves.

"What do you mean the fanzines are gone?" I asked Paladin.

"Stolen," she said softly.

"How is that even possible?" I asked.

She leaned back and raised her eyebrow, Spock-like. Paladin had taken that signature move from classic Trek and had turned it into a look filled with such disdain that nothing else I had ever seen rivaled it.

"I'm assuming they came in with a few boxes, packed up the fanzines, and walked out," she said. "Through this unlocked door."

I blushed. I often blush around Paladin. She unnerves me in a variety of ways.

"I didn't mean how did they steal it," I said, "although, come to think of it, that's a good question. We theoretically had state-of-the-art security here."

She started to respond, but I talked over her.

"I mean," I said, "how come you know about this and no one had bothered to tell me? I'm supposed to be running this show after all."

I sounded petulant. I hadn't meant to sound petulant, but I was. And a little worried. The Big Name Fan had entrusted us with his precious collection, and was monitoring the auction from his home in Texas. He and I both expected the fanzines to sell for nearly $200,000 all by themselves. After all, this was the perfect audience to overspend on famous fanzines. Or infamous fanzines. Or, rather, tiny mimeographed collectibles that no one outside our fannish family would give a rat's ass about.

"I'm telling you now," Paladin said in her most no-nonsense voice. That voice told me she was on the job. Which meant that the convention had hired her (*hired* her!) to find the fanzines, because they didn't want me to know about the theft.

Paladin wasn't well known for recovering stolen items at conventions. She called herself a bulldozer. She specialized in finding kidnap victims or saving kids from pedophiles or secreting abused family members out of truly bad situations. Which, come to think of it, was probably how Paladin had known Witt. She had probably partnered with him on many of the rescues being recounted in the gigantic function space behind us.

"How long have the fanzines been gone?" I asked.

Paladin's eyes narrowed. She took her job very seriously. I would never be able to get the details of this hire out of her, unless someone fessed up to me later.

"Paladin," I said. "I need to know. We advertised those fanzines."

As if that was the worst thing. It wasn't. There were dozens of other worst things that I was already making up.

"They were in place when the doors opened this morning," she said.

She was right. I would have noticed if they had vanished. I had done a very slow walk-through before the doors opened, eyeballing everything, although my eyeballs were a bit dry and sleep-deprived. I had been up until 4 a.m. the night before, setting everything up, and even with that I'd been too wired to sleep. So my eagle-eyes had probably been less eagle and more mole-like.

"So the fanzines were taken while people were here?" I asked, trying to make that compute. I hadn't arrived with the crowds, I hadn't seen how they had chosen their seats, I hadn't seen what Deggs had done from the start.

I also hadn't checked the doors around the room, like the one Paladin and I had just gone through.

"I don't know," Paladin said. "We have security footage, but that part of the room is dark."

It wasn't dark. It was dim. And I had set it up that way because I didn't want the artificial lighting to ruin the fanzines, some of which hadn't seen daylight in nearly fifty years. Deggs had complained. He had said that people needed to see the items clearly.

But he had complained about the fact that the fen attending couldn't pick up the fanzines and thumb through them. The very idea made me shudder. What if someone creased a page? Made a micro-tear? Deggs had run dozens of auctions, but he clearly wasn't a collector. A tiny crease in a page could cost us hundreds, by bringing down the price.

That was why I had insisted on keeping the fanzines, as well as the comics and other truly valuable paper collectibles, in cases. No one could touch them, except the organizers. And I, personally, had bought each and every person working this auction their own pair of gloves for handling the material.

I also put cotton glove boxes, filled to the brim with the cheap gloves that you sometimes found in libraries, so that no one would get their sweaty, chocolate-covered fingers on any of the collectibles. Anyone who wanted to touch *anything* had to put on a glove first.

Yes, I had said to Deggs when he complained about that too, I knew it wasn't common at convention auctions. But this was *Witt's* auction with some truly high-end collectibles, and I wanted to make sure we did it right.

"Which security footage were you using?" I asked.

"What do you mean, which security footage?" Paladin asked.

I closed my eyes just for a half-second. They were so tired, they wanted to stay closed. I didn't blame them. I was weary—first from handling Witt's estate along with my own work, and from this auction.

I opened my eyes to see Paladin staring at me, a crease in her forehead. I liked to think that crease was concern for me, but it might simply have been her puzzling over the security footage.

"They should have brought you in right from the start," she said, the crease getting deeper. "I told them that."

An exhausted anger flared in me. I almost lashed out, but I knew this wasn't Paladin's fault. I'd be talking to the convention organizers when this was all over.

"Why didn't they?" I asked.

She tilted her head a little. Her mouth opened, then closed, and then that crease turned into a full-blown frown.

"I, um…They…um…" She shook her head slightly. Paladin was not good at subtle. And she couldn't finesse anything. "Ah, hell. I hear you've been a bit difficult lately, Spade."

Difficult? *I* had been difficult? *Me?* With all the organizing and the work and the crap I had to do to get Witt's estate in order, the people fighting me on every turn, *I* had been the difficult one? *Me?*

I started to say all of that and then actually heard it. In my head. Actually heard it. The clear definition of difficult. I usually worked well with others. I didn't fly off the handle. I didn't use my sharp tongue as a weapon the way Witt had. I rarely attacked anyone, unless attacked first.

"Point taken," I said.

She raised her eyebrows just a bit. Apparently she had seen my mental change of course.

I needed to get my ego out of all of this and get to work. Fast.

"When and how did they bring you in?" I asked.

"About an hour into the memorial," Paladin said. "I was standing in the back and they pulled me into the hallway."

About an hour in. Fifteen minutes before I showed up.

"Were the belly dancers in the hallway out front here?" I asked.

"No," she said. "They were waiting in the kitchen."

Then she made a face as she realized that this door had been unlocked right from the start. And probably unlocked by the very people I had tasked with keeping it locked at all times.

It was my own fault. I had trusted the convention committee with a lot of this stuff, rather than the usual security team. I had worked the security team to death in the days before the convention, guarding the shipments, making sure that someone was at the door at all times.

Which meant that whoever had taken the fanzines had known that the A team had guarded the stuff *before* the auction started. The question was, had they known it because this was a so-called inside job or because they had walked the hallway and tried to get in from the start.

"You thought of something," Paladin said, as if that was a surprise.

I had thought of a lot of somethings, none of which I was ready to share.

"I need my computers and all the security footage you can find," I said to her.

"Where will you be?" she asked.

I wanted to be in the room, monitoring the auction, but I needed my Tower of Terror.

"Con Ops," I said, and headed that way.

———

No matter what convention I was at, Con Ops—convention operations—always smelled the same by Saturday. A combination of old pizza, spilled soda, and dirty feet. By Sunday, throw in some gamer-level B.O. and a hint of rotting bananas, and you had the stench that would take Con Ops to the Dead Dog party and beyond.

No one worked Con Ops for the entire convention straight. A rotating compliment of SMoFs (Secret Masters of Fandom) and local fen moved in and out of the room, constantly doing their jobs and overseeing everything they possibly could. At this moment, only three people sat in Con Ops, buried deeply in some work particular to them.

Usually, I lived in Con Ops during any convention I was a part of, but this BigCon wasn't usual. I had never been so deeply involved in a charity auction before, and I hoped I would never be again.

Still, I had set up my Tower of Terror in its usual spot on the side of the very large room. My computer system, which had only grown larger and more elaborate as most people's computers had grown smaller, looked intimidating. It should: I had encryption hardware on it that rivaled the best Silicon Valley firms. In fact, I had consulted at more than a few of them, and helped them with their designs, particularly for their financial protocols.

In front of the Tower of Terror sat my chair. No one but me touched my chair. My chair had more buttons and levers than a Navy destroyer. And it was set up to my specifications, so on that level, I would know if someone monkeyed with it.

Although there was one person known to monkey with it— and that was Paladin.

I sat down gingerly, just in case she had changed something. But she hadn't. Then I grabbed three laptops. I had placed several hidden cameras near all the collectibles. I had also placed several visible cameras around the auction. The visible camera feed ran to a small laptop that I kept in the auction room, as well as to the cloud so that I could access them from anywhere.

I had wanted people to know they were being watched. But I also wanted them to relax a little, and to believe that those visible cameras were the *only* cameras.

The hidden cameras fed into one of my clean laptops. There was nothing else on that laptop. I grabbed it and rewound the feeds on that too. If I needed to, I would combine the hidden and the visible camera feeds on a third laptop and see what it told me.

I focused on the visible cameras first. I studied the area near the fanzines. Yeah, it was dark, but I had set up two different kinds of visible cameras there—a regular one and an infrared. I moved the imagery from the regular camera forward slow enough that I could see everything, but not so slowly that it ran in real time.

Sure enough, about twenty minutes into the memorial, someone dropped a white glove over the camera itself. I reversed the image and slowed it down, going frame by frame, hoping to see whoever had done this. But no one appeared.

Whoever had done it had known how to stay out of camera range.

Once I determined that I couldn't see the person from the visible camera, I fast forwarded quickly, waiting until someone peeled the glove off the camera. That had come forty-five minutes in when a member of the concom discovered the missing fanzines.

I let out a soft whistle, annoyed that it had been so very easy. Then I went back and watched the imagery of the glove covering the camera again. There was no hand, nothing, no sideways shot of flesh or a fingernail or anything. Not even any movement.

So, I rewound the infrared to that exact moment, and compared frame by frame. I saw a lot of movement far away, but no heat signature close enough to drop that glove over the camera.

That irritated me.

So I got up, grabbed a Coke, stared at the untouched veggie platters on the snack table, and grabbed cheese and crackers instead. I hoped I wouldn't be here long enough to regret failing to order a pizza.

I ate the cheese and crackers quickly, cleaned off my hands, and then went back to work, dragging my Coke with me. I didn't sip it though. I stared at it for a moment, thinking about Witt's death. Then I set the unopened Coke back in the bucket of ice, and pulled out a bottle of water instead.

Small steps. Small, small steps.

I returned to my chair, and opened the other laptop. This time I examined the footage from all the hidden cameras. I started with the cameras closest to the fanzines. None were really close to the fanzines. I figured no one would want to steal those. My mistake.

No one dropped any gloves or coverings on the hidden cameras. Apparently, no one had seen them, which was as I intended.

I watched, but couldn't see anyone near the table at all as the glove fell onto the visible camera.

Then I reversed the footage from the hidden cameras. Yep, I got four different views of that glove floating onto the table, but none of anyone standing *in front of* the table.

I cursed in Klingon.

At that moment, Paladin entered Con Ops with a flash drive in her hand.

"Hotel security," she said. "Including some stuff they didn't want to hand over."

Then she gave me a feral little smile. I was glad I hadn't been in the room with her when she got this.

I took the flash drive, and opened one of the air-gapped laptops. I didn't want any virus or program leaching into my systems or into the systems for Con Ops. I'd learned the hard way that hotel systems, particularly those of hotels at various science fiction and comic conventions, had some of the most creative viruses.

There were four hotel security cameras in that large auction room, because that room had initially been four large ballrooms. Usually they were separated by walls that the hotel could break down for bigger groups. No one noticed those walls, not even in their absence. One camera for one room.

But I didn't want to see the images from those four cameras. Not yet anyway. As I was downloading the footage onto the air-gapped laptop, I went to the one with the visible cameras and opened the security footage from one of the cameras faraway, a camera that faced the fanzines.

On that footage, they looked dark. I had set up the cameras before I laid out the items up for bid, so I went all the way back to the beginning of the footage, days ago, when the only people in the hotel had been me and the concom.

"Who're you looking for?" Paladin asked, startling me. I had forgotten she was there.

It wasn't often I forgot Paladin. She wasn't the forgettable type. But I'd been so wrapped up in my work...

"I'm checking my memory," I said, not answering her directly.

Finally, I got to the moment after the cameras were set up. The tables were in place, but the chairs weren't. Some of the hotel staff was putting them out. The bang-slap of metal chairs being opened echoed throughout the footage.

I zoomed in as much as I could on the empty table with its standard issue hotel table cloth. Black, like we had requested, because black showed off the goods better than almost any other color. And it didn't reflect the light.

I wasn't looking at the table or the cloths, though. Nor was I looking at the people.

I was staring at that back wall.

It wasn't a wall. It was a collapsible wall.

Which surprised me just a little, because we hadn't been given the option of expanding lengthwise. We were able to open between the various rooms—width wise—but not the back.

"What's behind that wall?" I asked Paladin.

"Nothing," she said.

"Something," I said. "That wall's one of the collapsible ones."

"Only there, though," she said. "Look."

Her fingertip touched the imagery. She was right. The collapsible wall only ran the length of that particular ballroom— one of the side ballrooms, as far from the kitchen as possible.

"Do we have footage from behind that so-called wall?" I asked.

"Not that I saw," she said.

"Would you do a walk-around for me?" I asked.

"A what?" she asked.

"Get hotel security to take you back there, and see whatever it is that's behind that wall."

"Spade," she said in a cautious tone. "Hotel security doesn't like me very much right now."

"Can you do this computer work?" I asked.

"I don't even know what *this computer work* is," she said.

I nodded. I knew she didn't.

"Then, Obiwan," I said, "you are our only hope."

She glared at me. "You don't look like Princess Leia." she said half under her breath.

"Then I'm in good company," I said. "Because Carrie Fisher doesn't look like her either."

Paladin gave me one of those looks, the one that suggested I had crossed some kind of line.

"I prefer General Leia Organa," she said.

"I prefer solving this before the thief has too much of a head start on us," I said, turning my chair so that I could urge her to get out of the room.

But she was already gone.

———

I got lost in footage, ghost images, and infrared visions. Normally, I would have combined all of the footage into one gigantic master-piece, but I didn't have time. Besides, I didn't want to merge files that could end up compromising each other.

Fen knew a lot about computers, and I was just paranoid enough to worry that the theft of the fanzines was the kind of thing that someone would use to set me up and load a virus on my Tower of Terror. After all, that someone had to know that I would be involved. They also had to know that I would use hotel security camera footage to find the thief.

And they might know that the footage could be downloaded on a flash drive with tons of memory. They might think I was incautious enough to insert a strange flash drive into the Tower of Terror.

They, of course, would be wrong.

I had so many little screens open on my laptop screen that I wondered if this was what a fly felt like, viewing all kinds of things at once. I had learned how to process that much information coming at me at one time, and most of it didn't even register.

So when I saw the darkness around the fanzines grow on several of my security feeds, I didn't discount it as a glitch. Instead, I slowed the relevant feeds down, used a program in some video software to see if anything had changed in the recording (it hadn't), and then looked to see what exactly had changed.

Some of the small lights I had installed far from the fanzines, but close enough to add to the ambient light, had shut off.

Deliberate, and traceable.

I made a mental note, and continued viewing the footage. Something moved ever so slightly behind the table. I caught that on several feeds as well.

Then the glove floated down from the back, its whiteness catching the light.

I wondered how people missed this, so I brought up the sound on one of the camera feeds—and recognized the voice that was speaking.

It belonged to aging pin-up girl, Delilah Danvers, whose entire career had been about her looks and her...um...assets. The fen kept her alive, going from convention to convention, autographing 1950s cheesecake photos, and all of the art that she had inspired. She was famous in fandom, but not really famous anywhere else, not any more.

And she was sobbing her way through a story about Witt. Seemed he had helped her too, keeping her house from being fore-closed and inviting her to her first convention in 1980 or so, starting the revival of her "pin-up" career.

I realized, as I was startled by her voice, that I hadn't been watching the feed either. I had been listening to that incredibly riveting tale. I rewound the footage, not liking the idea that had come to me, that Delilah was somehow involved in this.

The woman who had sobbed like that wouldn't have been willing to steal from the auction, would she?

I accidentally rewound that footage too far, and hit *start* (yeah, okay, she got to me), and another voice—this one belonging to Groot, a SMoF friend of mine—shook and broke as he recounted the way that Witt had gotten Groot to the hospital and paid for his care after he was nearly beaten to death by some anti-gay bigots in the 1990s.

Okay. That stopped me too. It wasn't that Groot or Delilah were involved in the theft. It was the memorial itself. The thief either took advantage of the heartrending stories as a spur of the moment thing or the thief had gambled that people would be too upset to notice.

Or maybe he simply thought that no one would care about the fanzines. I had certainly thought so, or I would have put more protection around them. I had them there for a specific kind of collector. I hadn't expected the general public to be interested.

I moved the footage forward to that moment where the lights went dim and went frame by frame in several different security feeds. In one, I finally saw what I had been looking for.

The back wall didn't just fold back. It was composed of large square panels. Apparently they could be removed too, because one slid out of the way. A black-clad arm ending in a fist emerged from the back. The fist almost reached the visible cameras when it opened, releasing the glove. It went back and did the same thing on the other visible cameras, all within thirty seconds.

Never mind. This had been planned at least since we attached the memorial to the auction.

Once the cameras were covered, both hands emerged, along with the silhouette of a slight figure. The person quickly piled up the fanzines—the ones that were scattered in front of the visible cameras—and then eased them back. They disappeared into the opening in the wall.

Then the hands emerged one more time, grabbing the Lucite cases that held the most valuable fanzines, and sliding them into the back.

I finally understood why the lights had to be dimmed. The

movement of those cases would have reflected nearby light, no matter how small, and made the move visible.

But it had barely been visible. The cases disappeared into the hole, then the panel went back into place.

The fanzines were gone—and it had taken less than three minutes.

"Wow," I said, impressed in spite of myself. If this wasn't a professional job, then it was the closest thing I had ever seen.

Which made my stomach knot up. Because I had no idea how we were going to catch a professional thief of this quality.

Then "The Ballad of Paladin" blared in Con Ops.

I picked up my cell phone with shaking hands. "Yeah?" I said.

"Good job, Spade," Paladin said. "We found the fanzines."

I blinked, going from despair to confusion in one quick second. "What?"

"They were exactly where you said they'd be," she said. "In the back behind the wall. You want me to put them back out?"

I was so confused I almost said yes. But something was wrong here. Why pull the fanzines back and not take them away? To store for later, so they could be easily removed under cover of darkness? But wouldn't it have been better to move them when no one knew they were gone?

This wasn't making sense to me.

"I'll be right there," I said, as I hung up and tucked the cell in my pocket.

————

The back area behind the fanzine table was smaller than I expected. There was barely enough room for me, the fanzines, and Paladin. A hotel security guard stood just outside, shifting from foot to foot as he waited for us.

Apparently, this hotel had been through a new remodel each time it got new owners—and it had had new owners ten times in the last fifteen years. This space was clearly supposed to be storage, but it had gotten blocked by metal kitchen shelves.

Paladin had showed me the fingerprints in the dust and dirt, where someone had moved the shelving unit to reveal this dark space. I was leery of all of it, considering the spider webs and the centuries of dirt. Someone had to have known that this space was here in order to use it. There was no way anyone would have stumbled on it.

Paladin was using a gigantic square flashlight, the kind police organizations used to illuminate big unlit spaces. I had no idea where she got it. It revealed even more dirt and grime, and a cleared-out area where the boxes were.

It also revealed handprints—or rather, glove prints—on a bunch of the fake wall panels. Apparently our Bad Guy had tried several of the panels to see if they worked.

Which meant that he (she?) had to have been here before, at least once, to know where everything was.

As I suppressed a sneeze at all the dust, I tried to remember when we designed the layout for all of the auction goods. Donations had continued to arrive as late as Wednesday, and all of them were really good. I had moved things around several times before Thursday morning.

I had had a lot of help, as well, most of it from volunteers and other SMoFs.

"Problem solved, right, Spade?" Paladin asked again. She glanced at the wall between us and the auction. I could hear Deggs' auction patter. It sounded like he was moving quickly.

"This is weird," I said, and put out a hand for the flashlight. She gave it to me. I inspected all parts of the back area. There were prints here, but I would wager they were glove prints, not hand-prints. And they were small.

Still, we had the fanzines back. I glanced at my phone. We were thirty minutes from the first break in the auction itself. We had several scheduled, with meals nearby. We couldn't work Deggs for twelve hours straight, but he wanted to handle the auction alone. So we had twenty-minute breaks built in, with food carts in the hallway at the ready.

"Let's get these zines out of here," I said. I wanted the fanzines in good light, to make sure that they weren't covered with dirt or ruined.

Paladin got some boxes from the storage area and put towels in the bottom without me even asking. She also brought me gloves, which I wouldn't have thought of until I bent over near the fanzines.

I slipped on the gloves and picked up the first stack of fanzines. I was worried that all this mishandling had ruined the bottom fanzine—that it was on a bare concrete floor, covered in dirt—but I should have known better. Someone had set down fresh wood strips, then covered them with pristine white sheets.

In my CSI TV imagination—which was all I had, since I was a forensic accountant, not a forensic tech—I figured some police department could trace the wood, the sheets, and maybe even those tiny handprints.

But none of that was my concern at the moment. My concern was the fanzines. I gingerly put them in the boxes that Paladin provided. Then I sent her for some extra Lucite protective cases. I knew we had emptied out a few in the course of the auction already. The old Lucite cases would remain here, in case I got a last minute urge to call the actual police.

We finally got everything packed. My back ached and I was covered in grime. Before I unpacked the fanzines, I would have to change clothes, although I knew that would be tough. I had barely fifteen minutes to get to my room, shower and put on grime-free clothing.

Somehow I made it, even though my back ached and demanded that I stay in the hot shower longer. I didn't listen. I changed into a SMoFcon T-shirt, some black jeans, and the only other pair of shoes that I had, and still made it back to the kitchen with three minutes to spare.

Paladin remained, covered in dirt and spider webs, sitting near the boxes like the fierce warrior she was.

"What are we doing next?" she asked.

"I'm carrying these into the function space and putting them out," I said. "You're getting kitchen and storage footage from hotel security from the past week. Also, see if they'll cough up the names of any current or past employees who knew about that room."

She blew a strand of hair off her forehead, and managed to dislodge a bit of spiderweb as well.

"You act like I made friends with the security staff," she said.

I smiled for the first time since she had told me about the theft. "Just tell them that if we don't figure out who did this, they'll be on the hook for hundreds of thousands in damages."

"What damages?" she asked. "We recovered everything."

"But we have no idea what condition it's in," I said. And that was half truthful. I wanted to be the one to put the fanzines back out because I wanted to see if any of them were ruined.

Behind the door, I heard the scraping of chairs and the sound of voices. Apparently Deggs had called the break.

"See you in fifteen," I said to her as I grabbed the nearest box.

I hoped fifteen was all I was going to need.

———

Half the concom, it seemed, wanted to help me put the fanzines back out. I sent them on their way. The only person I would have trusted to help me was Deggs and he was getting a bowl of the hotel's special Pho Ga, so that his throat would remain lubricated for the next several hours of work.

I put out the loose fanzines, shaking them gently just a bit in case dirt had fallen on them. I didn't inspect as closely as I normally would have, but they seemed fine.

Then I adjusted the fanzines in the Lucite cases. I finished with five minutes to spare. And looked at the nearest case.

Something was a little off. I had set up those cases in the first place, and there had been an even number of fanzines inside of each case. In the case nearest to me, there was an odd number of fanzines.

I felt my heart sink. I took my phone out of my pocket and scanned the fanzine list I had stored on it, comparing the truly valuable ones to the ones in the case.

Sure enough, one was missing. The thirteenth issue of *Goop, Grope, and Grimm.* I felt a little chill as I thought about the implications of that.

The room was growing louder. I turned around, scanning for Deggs. He had returned, carrying a bottle of some sports drink, which he (correctly) placed beneath his podium. Then he wiped off his hands and walked over to me.

"Well?" he asked.

"Save the fanzines until after the next break," I said to him. "I want to make sure they're laid out properly."

"Just glad we got them back," he said.

"Me, too," I said. I stayed near the table as he got the auction back under way.

I scanned the crowd. A sea of familiar faces, and some not so familiar ones. Plus a lot of familiar names, who looked a lot

older than they should have. The graying of the fen commenced
apace.

I was pretty convinced that the person who had stolen the
fanzine was somewhere in this room. I also suspected that person
hadn't left their chair during the theft itself.

I was looking for someone who had either worked here or run
a con here back in the day. This hotel complex had long been a
home for BigCon. I knew I was looking for a longtime fan,
someone who would have been on any one of a dozen lists I had
mailed or emailed information to.

I was also looking for someone with money—because they
had hired muscle to steal the fanzine. I suspected that muscle had
no idea about collectibles—except what our Bad Guy had told
them—which told me that the Bad Guy didn't care about the
condition of *Goop, Grope, and Grimm*, because simply grabbing it
wrong could destroy it.

I listened as issue 25 of DC's *The Brave and The Bold*, which
had an early incarnation of Suicide Squad, sold for a ridiculous
$750. That outrageous competitive bidding was what I had hoped
for when I set up this auction.

Then I slipped out of the room, and quietly made my way to
Con Ops.

———

My Tower of Terror had an unofficial history of fandom inside its
databases. I'd been going to conventions long before I became a
Microsoft Millionaire, and I'd worked with concoms for decades.

I also understood patterns. That was why I was good with
numbers.

I knew now I was looking for a fan who had to be old enough
to have come to cons on his own in the early sixties, but young

enough at the time to have written something as unbelievably awful as "The Adventures of Morgana Jones." The fan was probably LA or Vegas based, with a parent who had worked either in the entertainment industry or was connected to the Mob somehow—or both.

I didn't have to look hard. As I said, our people had been dying in droves of late. The fen, most of whom did not exercise and ate to excess, rarely lived to see eighty. My database of candidates was now shockingly small.

I called Paladin. She needed to go, along with hotel security, and guard the door to a room on the 35th floor. She asked why and I wouldn't tell her, not yet.

I needed to make sure my hunches were correct.

I shut down the Tower of Terror and headed back to the auction. This time, I entered from the back of the room, and scanned until I saw the person I was looking for.

Dwight had moved his wheelchair near the *Star Trek* collectibles from the original series, some of which he had donated to this very auction. Dwight had been a good and generous member of fandom, always willing to donate to an auction or spend a thousand or two at a charity event that was falling short.

I approached him from his good side. He'd lost an eye in a freak accident as a child.

"Can we talk?" I asked as I bent down so that he could hear me.

He gave me a sheepish look, then backed his electronic wheelchair up. Together we headed into the hallway. It smelled of tacos and hotdogs and cinnamon rolls from the food trucks parked near the wall. I was hungry. Again.

But I was also focused.

"You could've just asked me for it," I said to Dwight. "I would have given you a special price. It probably would've been cheaper than stealing it."

His cheeks turned red. He bowed his head. He had lost most of his hair in the intervening years, except for a fringe around the back. He looked nothing like the man I had met at an early San Diego Comic-Con, back when the only people who attended were actual comic book fans. Back then he had been tall and thin, just like me. Now he outweighed me by at least a hundred pounds and had lost the use of his legs years ago.

He wouldn't be with us long either.

"I didn't want you to know I had it," he said.

"Why not?" I asked.

"Because," he whispered. "I was going to destroy it."

If I had been a true collector, I would have stepped back in horror. As someone who had been around collectors all my life, I still felt a deep shock.

"Why would you do that?" I asked, trying not to sound as judgmental as I felt.

"Because," he said, "it was the annotated version."

I had never heard of an annotated version. "What?"

He rubbed his left hand on the armrest of his wheelchair. His good eye actually teared up.

"Ike lied," he whispered.

It took me a moment to understand what he meant.

"In front of Congress?" I tried not to let my voice rise, but I wasn't sure I succeeded. The woman running the cinnamon bun food truck looked at us.

Dwight nodded. Then closed his eyes.

"He knew it was you?" I asked.

"Worse," Dwight said. "He knew about my dad."

His dad, William Dwight Weeks, who had been one of the first police officers on the scene at the Bugsy Siegel murder site in

Beverly Hills. The elder Weeks had quit his job with the police to work security, first in Cuba, and then in Vegas, and finally, at the studios. Apparently, he had never lost his mob connections.

"I don't understand," I said.

Dwight glanced at the food truck operators, and a fan who sat on a bench nearby, reading a battered copy of *Ancillary Justice*. Dwight drove further down the hall, so that no one could hear us.

"My dad," Dwight said after he stopped the wheelchair. "He was involved. He handled Oswald."

So the rumors *were* true. "And he knew Roddenberry," I said.

"Yeah," Dwight said. "They were drinking buddies."

"So, you had prior knowledge of the assass—"

"No," Dwight said. "No. Like any good fanzine, *Goop, Grope, and Grimm* was months behind schedule. It came out in January."

"Why would you write a story like that about your dad?" I asked.

He shook his head. "I didn't. Ike and I were best friends. I had to tell somebody, and I told him, to my everlasting regret."

I frowned.

"He wrote the story, Spade. He put it in the fanzine and left it on *my* doorstep. Fortunately, I found it before my dad."

"Why would Ike do that?" I asked.

"Money," Dwight whispered. "My family had money. And Ike wanted some of it."

"He was *blackmailing* you?"

Dwight nodded. "Until my dad found out that I was giving Ike money, although he never found out why. Threatened to cut off Ike's body parts one at a time if he ever spoke to me again. Apparently, Ike didn't know Dad was dead by the time he testified before Congress."

Dwight ran a hand over his face. I had never seen him so nervous. Or so upset.

"I thought the issue was closed after Ike died," Dwight said. "Especially when I heard that Ike's family had tossed out Ike's collection. I didn't know that particular copy of *Goop, Grope, and Grimm* still existed until I got your flyer."

"Still, Dwight, I would have given it to you if you asked," I said.

"But you might have looked at it," he said.

I frowned. "What's in that issue?"

His lips thinned. "A different version," he said. "With all the details."

"Your dad's gone," I said. "Why not just turn the story over to the authorities? A lot of people wonder what really happened."

Dwight shook his head just a little. "I can't," he whispered. He seemed terrified.

"Dwight," I said. "It's been fifty-three years. Surely no one would hurt you or your family if this came out."

He bit his lower lip. Those tears still threatened.

"I can't risk it," he said.

I let out a breath. "It's in your hotel room, right?"

He grabbed my arm so tightly that he pulled the skin. "Spade, seriously. Don't pick it up. Don't touch it. Don't do anything with it. Please."

I thought about it for a moment. Who would believe an annotated version of a fanzine story from the 1960s held the key to the murder of JFK? I wasn't sure I did, even if Dwight's dad had been as mobbed up as the histories made it seem.

"Tell you what," I said. "You do two things. You tell me who you hired to grab the fanzine."

"Sure," he said a little too eagerly.

"And you pay the auction for the fanzine. Right now. No questions asked. Like you should have from the beginning."

"How much?" he asked.

I wasn't feeling as kind as I usually did. Who knew how high that thing would have gone in the bidding?

I knew what I had hoped the fanzine would bring. I named a price twice as high as that.

He looked a little pale. But his family had once had money. Maybe he still did as well.

"Okay," he said after a moment.

"Okay," I said. "But we're not done. We're going to checkout, and you're going to pay for the fanzine right then and there. Once the payment goes through, we'll give you the fanzine."

"Don't read it, Spade," he said.

I nodded, making no real promise at all.

———

I asked Paladin to photocopy the entire fanzine in the business center, and then hold onto the fanzine until Dwight's funds cleared. I had her hand me the photocopy, and she gave him the fanzine.

Which he burned in front of us.

I read the story days later. It had footnotes, and a lot of names, all of which had been in the Warren report on the assassination and were also mentioned at the House Select Committee on Assassinations.

Dwight had been blackmailed for nothing.

His dad had worked *security*, as in *security guard*, not as in one of the inner circle of any of the mobbed up groups he'd been near. From everything I could gather, with twenty-twenty hindsight, his dad had been one of those little men who tried to make himself more important than he actually was.

Although, this theory nagged at me a bit. I did some digging and never really could figure out where the family money came from.

Not that it mattered. Dwight died several months later. The thief, Rose Beetum, a young gamer who thought she was doing a live-action role with her favorite character, was banned from West Coast conventions for five years, although I suspected that wouldn't stick.

And the auction went off well enough that we were only fifty thousand short of the matching funds goal, which shocked the heck out of me. I got some Big Name Fans to put up the rest of the money, and we made a huge donation to Witt's favorite charity, marked—as per his wishes—Anonymous.

Witt would have loved it. All of it.

Intrigue, presidential conspiracy theories, collectibles. I found it fascinating that things so important to the fen—fanzines and storytelling—probably would have made no difference to investigators in the decades-old assassination saga. Maybe it would have made a difference in the 70s, though, when the people involved were still alive. But I doubt that.

Although I did mail a copy, anonymously, to the FBI, not that it mattered. The FBI had been embroiled in controversies of its own for the past year, and probably didn't have time for old conspiracies. I never heard anything from anyone.

Which probably would have pleased Witt as well.

I think about him a lot, even though I'm done with the estate. I miss him more than I thought possible.

Ever since the auction, people ask me if I have a Witt story. I always smile and say I have a lot of them. They insist, trying to probe to see if I have the kind of Witt story that everyone told at the memorial.

I do have one. It involves those dark days before I got my high-powered Microsoft job, when I thought I was alone in the world, and I had nearly lost hope.

But I had promised Witt I would never tell anyone what he did.

And I keep my promises.

Every single one of them.

In memory of Bill Trojan

THE CASE OF THE STOLEN MEMORIES

A SPADE CONUNDRUM

He brought them with him, his old friends. Every convention, Ira Hartmann carted his Kodak Carousel slide projector and hundreds of slides into the suite he had sweet-talked the con com into providing for him. Ira was a member of First Fandom, an organization founded in 1959 to bring together science fiction fans of the "golden era"—the pre-1938 era.

Why 1938? Because of the Great Worldcon War of 1939. At least, that was what Ira called it, and I had adopted the terminology, because I'd first learned about the 1939 Worldcon first from him.

My name is Spade. I've been around fandom long enough that most people believe I know everything about everything fannish, but I don't. I am just old enough to have spanned a couple of eras. I knew a lot of members of First Fandom, and I also knew people who should've been in First Fandom, and I knew writers from the Golden Age, and I knew writers from just a few years ago.

Most folks would not say I'm a sensitive soul, but I kinda sorta am. I knew that there were topics the First Fandom folks did not like discussing. Ask Ira about the Exclusion Act at NY Con 1 (as its detractors called that first Worldcon), and he'd give you a sad look. Then he'd change the subject and happily tell you about how he was standing outside the "pavilion" when he spied "this kid from California," who just a few years later would "become" Ray Bradbury.

To hear Ira tell it—all of it—those early years, the 1930s, were glorious. Yeah, they were kids, and no, they didn't have money, but they all loved each other and they all loved science fiction, and *Hey, Spade, look at what we built, kid. Look at what we built.*

What they built. A network of conventions that had been going around the country ever since that very first Worldcon in 1939, a gathering place for people who loved science fiction, people who loved reading and books and movies and games and all kinds of things that were shunned back in Ira's day.

Ira's day. I was never really certain what Ira's day was. The man was impressive as hell. He was an ambitious talker—probably an annoying one in 1939. He'd been fifteen that year when he met some of the most important people in his life. He became an agent for some of them—I like to imagine this punk kid, talking to big-time editors all of whom I imagine looked like Perry White in the oldest of the old Superman comics—square-jawed, loud-talking, salt-and-pepper hair and a take-no-guff persona.

Yeah, kid, yeah. But tell me, kid, why ya think we should waste ink on that *story, huh?*

Come to discover, years later, that the editors Ira was selling stories to weren't much older than Ira himself. In fact, some of them ran that first Worldcon, and a couple of them might've caused the split heard 'round fandom.

I don't know all the details because I don't *want* to know all the details. Most of the folks involved were friends of mine—

elderly friends of mine who would stiffen up whenever anyone mentioned that first Worldcon.

All those years later, it was still a source of great pain. Hell, during one of the First Fandom Hall of Fame Award presentations at a Hugo ceremony in the '90s, the two factions almost came to blows—and we're not talking young people. We're talking people in their sixties and seventies screeching at each other about something that happened *decades* ago.

I'd been working security that night. I had to pull two men apart before they broke bones in their hands trying to punch each other. Still, they both ended up with black eyes and one might've lost a tooth or two.

There's a lot of dirt back there, stuff I don't want to know about my heroes. I watched too many of them grow clay feet over the years. Some because of their boorish behavior and some because of stories about them that I simply can't get out of my head.

Modern SF has epic wars, but most of them are online now. I try to avoid them. Back in the day, though, the stuff got hashed out in person. Or in APAzines (amateur press association mimeographed fan magazines). Or in rumor and innuendo.

It was as bad then as it is now. It just didn't happen quite as fast. It didn't go from incident to kerfuffle to picking sides to hatred in the space of a few hours. Usually it took weeks, sometimes months.

Yeah, fandom stuff can get serious. And it lasts. The friendships last, and the enemies last.

Ira knew that. He did his best to avoid the controversies. I can imagine scrawny little Ira, talking his way past all the "older" members of what would become First Fandom, ducking punches and deciding to placate the feelings of others, probably doing it with an overflow of words.

Ira was always overflowing with words—except that morning.

That morning, I saw an Ira hardly anyone saw. Maybe his wife, back when she'd been alive. Maybe a couple of his friends. Maybe.

He had been sitting on the bed in his suite, hands on both sides of his head, body hunched. He wouldn't answer when anyone talked to him, and finally Doris Xavier, who'd been running con security, sent for me, thinking maybe I knew who his family was.

When someone hits their eighties, which Ira was that day, folks suspect severe illness before they think of anything else, which I think of as not all that fair, really, particularly as I age.

That morning—that case. I don't talk about it.

Or I didn't.

But Ira's gone now. SF isn't quite the same as it was. Half the eras that I spanned are no longer there. I'm inching into the older generation and I gotta tell you, it's weird.

In those years, Eschercon took place in April. They moved it when a larger convention—with comics and movie stars and some really good cosplay—kept eating away at their membership.

But April—not really the best month to hold a convention in Upstate New York. Either we'd have snow or slush or ice or some damn storm that would delay arrivals. Except the locals who knew which train to take, and who didn't mind getting picked up at the train station by a fan who couldn't drive worth a damn.

I always flew in, because at the time I lived in Seattle proper. I'd made my millions from Microsoft (I'm one of the original Microsoft millionaires), the Victorian I'd bought near the university had quadrupled in value, and I had only just started thinking of selling it.

I'd actually considered going to NY, because so many of my fannish friends lived there. So I was working as many NY conventions as I could, getting to see the back parts of towns that no one normally saw.

The hotel where Eschercon was in those years was the strangest hotel I'd encountered—at least to that point. The local fen (the fannish plural for fans) called it the Escher Hotel, and it was how the con got its name.

The Escher Hotel was really three hotels mashed together. You'd walk down a hallway on the fourth floor and suddenly the carpet would change color and according to the signage you'd be on the eighth floor. Stairways led nowhere, and the third floor rooms in one part of the hotel would dead-end into a blank concrete wall which had once been the outside wall of one of the mashed-up hotels.

To make things even weirder, the hotels stood on a definitive corner, where three (former) villages met. That intersection was the place where street names and zip codes changed. Each hotel was in a different village, and to this day, I have no idea what village the intersecting parts of the hotel(s) stood in.

That year, Ira's suite was on the top floor of the newest hotel, where the guests of honor were staying. I had a suite on that floor too, not because I was special, but because I had money to burn, so I burned it—at least at conventions. I believed in comfort more than anything else. Still do.

So it didn't take me long to get to Ira's room. Doris was hovering at the door, looking nervous, and some sweet young fan, a pretty girl of a type that Ira always seemed to attract, hovered with her.

The sweet young fans, as Doris and I called them, were arm candy for Ira. He was still stubbornly faithful to the wife he'd married at nineteen, and who had died of some awful cancer twenty years before. But he liked to pretend he was a ladies' man, and maybe, by his gentlemanly standards, he was.

"What's going on?" I asked as I barreled through the door.

Forgot to tell you that I'm more Nero Wolfe than Sam Spade. I'm not fond of orchids and I do leave my house and I don't have an assistant named Archie who runs into danger, but I am large and imposing and I like my creature comforts more than I like dishing out a punch.

I don't usually barrel either, but someone had said there was a problem with Ira, and for Ira, I barreled.

Doris stepped to one side and the sweet young fan looked at me like she'd never seen a fat man run before.

"I can't get Ira to tell me what's wrong," Doris said, sounding worried. Doris never sounded worried. That's why I liked working with her.

I glanced at the sweet young fan, about to tell her to go somewhere else, when I realized she was rubbing her hands together. Apparently, that gesture is called wringing, although for the life of me, I've never understood it.

"I came to get him for brunch," she said. "The door was open."

Her voice got a little louder, a little more insistent. Someone had probably already questioned whether or not she had spent the night in the room.

Ira never fought the perceptions of his manliness, unless it got the sweet young fen in trouble. Then he was Sir Galahad, ready to ride in on a metaphorical horse.

"I called his name, and he didn't say anything." She bit her lower lip. "I went in farther, and there he was."

She waved a hand at the bedroom, and my heart clenched. At that moment, I hadn't seen Ira yet, didn't know that he was hunched, didn't know that he was even alive, although I figured Doris would've told me if he wasn't.

I pushed past the sweet young fan and barreled toward the

bedroom. I know CPR. I've had to use it, but I was afraid to use it on Ira. He was still a small man, and in his eighties, he had become frail.

I wasn't sure I'd be able to do the compressions without shattering a bone.

But I didn't need to. Ira sat on the edge of his bed, his head bowed, his shoulders shaking, clearly alive.

I let out a gusty sigh of relief and walked over to him. I put my meaty hand on his shaking shoulder and said, "Ira, it's Spade."

He didn't acknowledge me.

That was when I realized he was crying. And, as I looked around the room, I noted that the bed was made, and the old fashioned he'd brought with him for a nightcap the night before was still sitting, untouched, on the nightstand. The ice had melted long ago, the bitters had settled on the bottom, and the whiskey wasn't that golden anymore, given the amount of water now in the glass.

Ira used drinks like that to help him sleep—or so he said—and I'd watched him down plenty before turning in. Ira was from that generation: he was a drinker, and proud of it.

I crouched. My knees cracked so hard I thought they probably heard the snap in New Jersey. I peered up at him. His hair, usually manicured away from his face with some sickly sweet gel, had fallen across his cheeks. His hands looked glued to his skin.

"Ira," I said again. "Ira, look at me."

He didn't. He wouldn't. I wasn't even sure he saw me.

I turned, straining my back. I would never get out of this position again, I was sure of it.

"Doris," I said none too loudly, because she was hovering near the door, the sweet young fan behind her, "call 911."

"No." The word was barely audible. A croak, really.

I looked back at Ira. He still hadn't pulled his hands away from his face, but he was sitting up a bit straighter.

"I'm okay," he said, even though it was clearly a lie.

He finally let his hands drop. His large nose was red, his eyes were puffy, and his cheeks were chapped.

His lower lip trembled, and that's when I realized he'd been crying. Crying for hours. The kind of crying that people did when someone died.

"Spade, you stay." Then Ira attempted a smile, maybe even one of his charming smiles, and said to the sweet young fan, "Honey, I'm skipping brunch, okay?"

"You sure?" she asked. "I mean, food would probably help—"

His smile had a bit of an edge now. I saw the Ira who had become a big Manhattan lawyer, who had given up fandom to negotiate deals in TV and theater when New York City was the center of the entertainment universe.

He had only come back to us after he retired and his wife died. And then he never mentioned all the things he had done in the name of entertainment. Just what he had been doing in SF before he had Become Somebody.

"Honey," he said in a way that made it clear that right now, he couldn't remember her name, "don't you worry about me."

She didn't notice. She was still hovering. It didn't matter how pretty or seemingly normal fen were, they were still fen. And there were reasons she was in the SF crowd. Apparently her inability to read a room was one of them.

I turned even farther so I could give her hand signals that I hoped she could understand. *He's okay* and *Go away*. I didn't quite make a shooing motion, but I almost did.

Doris took pity on her. Or on me. Doris took the sweet young fan by the arm and helped her out of the room as if she was the one in trouble, not Ira.

Then Doris pulled the door closed, and I collapsed onto the floor. My knees were not meant to hold all four hundred pounds of me in a crouch for that long.

Ira frowned at me.

"You okay?" he asked with a bit of an edge. On the one hand, it was typical Ira. He was concerned for someone else, always, wanting the best for people, always, but on the other hand, it was Ira the Lawyer. *You okay, because I gotta situation here.*

"Just needed to plant my butt on the floor," I said as if I did that every day.

It actually got a small smile from him.

"Tell me what's going on," I said, and the small smile faded as if it had never been.

His lower lip started trembling again. "My slideshow. It's gone."

My turn to frown. "Did you leave it somewhere?"

"Yeah," he said. "Here. In this room. I already did the show, Spade. You didn't come."

"I'm sorry," I said automatically. That tone—slightly blaming, slightly accusing—reached into a part of me that had once been smaller and less sure of himself. My mother used to use a tone like that when she had been disappointed in me, and that's what it felt like now, with Ira.

He waved a hand as if my lack of attendance didn't matter, even though it clearly did.

I wasn't going to tell him the truth, not about that. I only caught every third show that Ira did at conventions, because mostly, they were the same—Ira walking down memory lane, telling stories that were fascinating the first three or four times. The show was best when we were in a place like New York, which had First Fandom members heavy on the ground, and they could fight or argue or challenge Ira's memories. Or add to them.

I learned a lot about the early days of SF from those verbal tussles. He was right: I should have been at this one. I had forgotten all about it.

"It wasn't good," he said. "It got heated."

He always thought the contentious "shows" were the worst ones, primarily because they made him uncomfortable.

I had met the Hartmann clan on more than one occasion and when they got together, Ira's word was law. They all loved him—from the middle-aged adult kids down to the littlest of grandchildren—but no one disagreed with him.

I was pretty sure that the only place that anyone disagreed with Ira was in the tight little hotel rooms at various conventions, when his Kodak Carousel took center stage.

"And you're positive that you brought the entire show back to the room," I said, because I had to clarify.

"Spade, do I look like a *schlemiel* to you?" he snapped.

Since my only encounter at that moment in my life with the word *schlemiel* had been in the opening credits to *Laverne and Shirley*, and I never knew what it referred to, I figured this was not the time to guess. So I did not respond to the question exactly.

"Ira," I said. "I would ask the same thing of anyone. Sometimes we get distracted, especially if your panel was heated."

"It wasn't a panel," he said sullenly. "It was a presentation, and I got interrupted. *A lot.*"

He hated getting interrupted. He took the interruptions personally sometimes, as if people were discounting his memories. Longtime friends knew how to ask questions or volunteer their memories in a way that wouldn't anger him and derail the presentation.

"Who interrupted you?" I asked.

He waved a hand. "It's not important. What's important is that I got here, I put my equipment on that table over there—"

He continued to wave his hand, this time indicating the round table that most hotel rooms had as a "dining" table. This suite had an actual dining table in the very large living/dining/kitchen area, so this table was just an extra.

"—and then I went to dinner." He peered at me. "You remember dinner, right?"

It was a passive-aggressive jab, the kind I'd heard Ira use with his kids and some of his longtime friends, but never with me.

"It was a lovely dinner," I said. "Of course I remember it."

And if I didn't, my black American Express card would have reminded me at the end of the month in the form of a charge of $750 for the five of us who had been there.

"The soup could've been better," Ira muttered.

"It could have been," I said, mostly to get him back onto what actually happened.

"I had a drink with..." And he waved his hand again, this time to refer to the sweet young fan, whose name I couldn't remember either. "...and then I came back up here. *Alone.*"

He eyed me as if to reinforce the point. I knew he never brought the sweet young fen back for after-hours romping. I'd actually checked on Ira's activities with younger women. There weren't any. When I ran security at various conventions—something I hadn't done in a long time now—I made sure that whatever looked suspicious wasn't suspicious or criminal or had happened with consent.

With Ira, there was no need for consent, because he always walked the ladies to their doors—and left them there, in the hallway, before he toddled off to his own suite.

"You walked her home first, right?" I asked.

"Not last night," he said. "She retired early. I was talking to Ava Walters."

When Ira "talked" with Ava Walters, it was never really talking. It was shouting and fist-pounding and disagreements that could never be settled.

I'd seen photos of Ava back in the day, and she looked like Ava Gardner's not-quite-photo-ready sister. Same curvy figure, same big eyes. But Ava Walter's hair was always clumped or falling out of its pins, and she never did manage the art of makeup.

She had grown into a round woman who looked like someone's really nice mother (or grandmother these days) until you looked at her eyes. A glance from those eyes was enough to bring anyone to their knees.

She and Ira fought like cats and dogs all the time. But, from the things Ira said sideways when she wasn't in attendance, I got the sense that she was the one who got away.

"Did you settle anything?" I asked.

He glared at me. The look wasn't as powerful as usual, given his red tear-stained eyes.

"I had some new slides," he said. "She claims I mislabeled them."

"New slides?" I asked, unable to keep the surprise out of my voice. He hadn't had new slides in all the years I'd gone to the presentation. He had *different* slides, ones that would go in and out of the rotation, but never anything new.

"If you had come, you would've seen," he said.

"I'm sorry I missed it," I said, finally able to apologize with sincerity. Because I was sorry I missed the new slides. "What were they?"

"My son was cleaning out our basement," Ira said, "and he found an entire box I'd put there and forgotten about. I have *lots* of new slides."

I processed all of that information. Cleaning out the basement of old items in the house an eighty-five-year-old man had shared with his long-dead wife sounded more like cleaning out the house itself.

"And before you ask," he said, "yes, I'm moving. My son found me a place in his building."

His son lived in one of the newer condo complexes in Midtown. Very upscale and posh. I knew that Ira could afford it, but I was surprised. He had said he never wanted to leave the memories.

A shiver ran down my back. Maybe there was more to the tears than the lost Kodak Carousel.

"He insisted that I have a housekeeper come in every day." Ira's lips formed a thin line. "I guess he didn't like how the house was looking."

I gave him a sympathetic smile. "He wouldn't like how my house looks either, Ira."

Ira smiled at me, but it was perfunctory.

"So he's moving things, and found the slides," I said.

"And I've been labeling them," Ira said. "I'm going to donate everything when I go."

I knew that. He was having trouble finding a place for his memories, though. He'd thought of going to the newly established Science Fiction Hall of Fame, but it was too pro-focused for him. Even though the Hall of Fame was founded by a subset of fandom, they really didn't seem to respect the fannish community. And there were other problems as well.

I'd backed the project initially, but was seeing the nightmarish handwriting on a very political wall. So I stepped back. Ira had asked me a few times to help him find a university to take his things. I'd suggested the Eastern New Mexico University in Portales, but Ira made a face every time.

Which baffled me, because that collection was anchored by Portales resident Jack Williamson, who was also First Fandomeligible (whether or not he'd joined, I had no idea) and who was a decorated, important science fiction writer, who'd been published in every decade since the 1920s.

I never asked, although it seemed impossible to me that anyone would dislike Jack. I guessed, though, it was Portales or New Mexico. So far from the coasts and what Ira believed to be the Real World that I had a hunch he saw it all as also-ran.

"I brought out some of the new ones for the first time yesterday," Ira said. "I passed the word. You didn't get the word?"

I hadn't, but that didn't mean much. My attendance at cons was always more about running them in those days (heck, and in these days too) than it was about attending panels.

"I've been spending most of my time in Con Ops this convention," I said.

"You," Ira said, wagging a finger at me, "need a life."

I nodded, because I didn't want to disagree with him. I considered convention going and SF fandom my life. But Ira still believed in the 1950s American Dream. He thought I needed a wife to take care of my household and at least 2.5 kids.

I once made the mistake of telling him no woman would have me, and he spent the next con-year trying to fix me up with his sweet young fen.

"The slides," I said, trying to focus him on the problem. Trying to control a conversation with Ira was like trying to wrestle an aging but canny tiger.

He slid to the edge of the bed, so he could lean closer to me. His eyes actually lit up.

"They are of the 1939 Worldcon," he said. "They're *valuable*. My father gave me a Canon Rangefinder, and spent a small fortune, let me tell you."

Ira's father was one of the few who made money during the Depression. Ira would never tell me what his father did, but I looked it up. His father had a hand in the illegal alcohol industry and, like Joseph Kennedy, had entire boatloads (literal boatloads) of European booze ready to sell the night Prohibition ended.

"I spent another fortune in film," Ira was saying, "and developed it all after the convention."

He grinned. The grin relieved me more than I could say.

"People called me obnoxious because I was always sticking a camera in their face. That whole weekend. They kept calling me a pesky kid. One of them threatened to take the camera and smash it over my head."

I raised an eyebrow, Spock-like. "Do you remember who that was?"

"I wanna say it was Fred Pohl, because Fred had a lot of secrets, you know?" Ira said. "I'm not sure he was faithful to Leslie, even then. And he was a communist. You knew that, right?"

Fred Pohl was another of SF's most famous early writers. Fred's personal history was colorful to say the least. He had been married five times, and there were a lot of rumors about other women, particularly in the 1940s (when three of his marriages occurred). He had been a member of the Communist Party in the 1930s, when he was a teenager and renounced the party about the time of the first Worldcon. He went on to serve in an elite air unit in World War II, something I never heard him talk about.

Nor did he say much about his controversial years as a literary agent, although a lot of people hated him because of it. And his years as an editor.

Fred never showed up at any of Ira's talks, and I often wondered about their relationship. They never sat near each other, even when they were both in the greenroom at a con before a panel, and I didn't recall them ever exchanging words about anything.

It would make sense if their relationship was contentious. I sometimes saw the questionnaires that went to author guests, where they could ask to avoid other writers or fans, and Fred's had some really well-known names on them.

Ira never filled out one of the questionnaires because he only did his slideshow. He refused to sit on fannish panels, but that was something that only the Secret Masters of Fandom who ran conventions knew. Ira tried not to say anything bad about anyone at a convention, which made his comments about Fred—sideways as they were—unusual.

"You say you wanted to say it was Fred, but you're not saying it was Fred," I said. "Was it Fred?"

Ira shook his head. "I thought it was, the day it happened. But turns out it, it was Mervin DeGrastene."

That was a name I had never heard before.

"Who?" I asked.

"Nowadays you'd call him a Big-Name Fan," Ira said. "He was at every East Coast gathering before the war. And he looked a lot like Fred. Everyone said so. It really made Fred mad, too, because Fred got blamed for some of the things that Mervin did. When I think about it now, I wonder if Mervin encouraged the confusion."

I felt a little off-kilter. I had thought I knew everyone who had been part of science fiction in those early years. Or at least knew of them.

"What happened to him?" I asked.

"Mervin?" Ira frowned. "I don't know. I just stopped seeing him around."

"When?" I asked. "Before the war?"

"We all served, Spade. There was no during the war, and after..." Ira shook his head. "A lot of us became grown-ups after. Put away our childish things."

He gave me a sad smile. I knew part of this history, but I let him say it.

"Unfortunately, many of us saw SF as a childish thing," he said.

"Did you?" I'd never really asked him that before. I'd heard a number of reasons why he left fandom. Most people said it was because of his wife. She didn't approve at all.

He looked down at his hands. I looked at them too, twisted and swollen with arthritis. He saw my gaze and put them on his knees as if he was trying to stretch the fingers out.

"You don't know what it was like after," he said. "We built a peaceful world for you kids."

I waited. I'd heard that before. The world wasn't peaceful. I grew up in the Cold War, and it was scary. Small skirmishes and border wars always felt like they could spill into something much bigger and much more sinister.

But I was also aware that our generation had been spared the worldwide terror that had been the Second World War.

He shook his head, as if he was testing sentences and rejecting them.

Finally, he said, "Look, Spade. After the war, we, none of us, were the same. We'd seen things..."

I waited. His gaze still wasn't meeting mine.

"...and then there was the bomb. We did that. *Science* did that. Science wasn't this joyful benign thing anymore. I mean, even Jack Williamson came out of that war wondering how any of us could glorify science anymore."

I never thought of the early writers as glorifying science, although that was an element of SF from the beginning. Ira was right, though; 1950s' SF was decidedly darker than any we'd seen before, but that was true of every literary aspect of the 1950s. And movies too.

"So," Ira said, "a lot of us, we went on to other things."

So there it was, why Ira really left SF. It was easier to say that his wife forced him to do so. Pieces of Ira and parts of the stories he told fell into place now.

"The new slides," I said, changing the subject back. "They're all of the nineteen thirty-nine Worldcon?"

"No," he said. "But the ones I brought here are. They're from the local meetings and from the Worldcon and from just some of the get-togethers."

"And Ava was at those?" I asked.

He shook his head. "Not all of them."

"She angered you, though."

He gave me a sad smile. "She always angers me. I worry about you as a detective, Spade, if you haven't noticed that."

"Enough to be bothered by the interruptions at your presentation," I said.

"She approached me after the presentation," he said.

"So who interrupted you there?" I asked.

"Well, Sam," he said. "But Sam always interrupts me. He has to remain the authority on the history of SF, you know."

Again, with the bitterness. Which didn't surprise me with Ira's relationship to Sam Moskowitz. Sam was considered *the* authority on the early history of science fiction. He was the guy who barred several Futurians from entering the 1939 Worldcon. Sam. The authority.

The Futurians were a group of SF fans, many of whom ended up being truly influential in SF. People like Fred Pohl and Don Wolheim (who founded DAW books). Sam was a member of the Futurians until real-world politics got in the way. Most of the Futurians at that point were members of the Communist Party, which Sam did not like...or something like that.

As I said, I never did learn all the details. I liked all of these people, even the most contentious ones, and I'm educated enough to know that folks who flirted with Communism in the 1930s didn't really understand what the party was.

Especially teenage folks, which almost all of them were.

I never asked Ira which side of the great divide he fell on, but he probably wouldn't have told me anyway. But given the way he and Sam fought, I often wondered if Ira identified with the Futurians in that argument.

Although, in the 1950s, when Ira became a highfalutin lawyer, being affiliated with the Communist Party in any way was dangerous. And Ira had fingers in Hollywood, which meant he could have been called before the House Un-American Activities Committee if he so much as sneezed wrong.

I understood the caution then. Not so much now. Although I knew that the habits of a lifetime often became ingrained.

"Who else interrupted you?" I asked Ira.

He shrugged and looked down. I had never seen that kind of response from him before. He usually deflected a topic he didn't want to discuss by changing the subject.

"If you want me to find the carousel," I said, "then you need to tell me everything."

He raised his head, his eyes still lined with tears. "There is no everything, Spade. Some of us just disagree, is all. We've disagreed for sixty years. The fen were fighting when I left SF to go to war, and they were still fighting when I came back ten years ago."

"But it bothers you," I said.

"Yeah," he said quietly. "But not so much as Ava."

My legs were cramping up. I needed to get off this floor, but we had finally gotten to the meat of this discussion. I didn't dare move yet.

I waited. I wasn't sure if he was responding to "bother" in the literal sense or in the sense that she bothered a part of him that he didn't like to acknowledge after his wife's death.

"She says..." His voice trailed off and he looked down again.

When it became clear he wasn't going to say any more, I spoke for him. "She said that you didn't label everything properly on the new slides. Do you believe her?"

"*NO!*" He startled himself when he shouted, and actually scooted back a bit on the bed. "Sorry, Spade. Sorry."

It was clear from that kind of outburst that we were actually getting somewhere.

"What did she think you mislabeled?" I asked.

"If we had the slides, I could show you," he said.

"Do you still have the photos themselves?" I asked.

"Yes," he said. "Where'd you think I got the slides?"

"Are the photos here?" I asked.

His bushy eyebrows came together in a frown. "I had the slides. Why would I need the photos?"

I was groping at something. "Do other people know that you still have the photos?"

"I didn't say it, exactly," he said. "Not that it would've mattered to anyone. Sam thought the pictures were unimportant."

"But Ava didn't," I said.

"Oh, she didn't talk about importance," Ira said. "She pointed out—repeatedly, I might add—that I once again confused Fred with Mervin."

I tilted my head a little. "You'd done it before?"

"*No,*" Ira said. "She always thought I did, though."

"Why is that important to her?" I asked, mused, really. Then I saw the stricken look on Ira's face.

"Why? I thought you were a detective, Spade. All the little details in everything, they're the most important." Ira leaned back just a little. He had forgotten about the theft, at least for the moment, and that made him calmer.

"Fred doesn't come to your presentations," I said. "What about Mervin?"

Ira barked out a laugh. It wasn't a laugh at my expense or anything else. Instead, it was a laugh of surprise.

"I thought you knew fannish history, Spade," he said.

"I do," I said.

"Then you know that Mervin DeGrastene never made it to the war. He died in Queens about a month after that Worldcon." Ira lowered his voice. "Everyone thinks he was murdered."

There was a lot to unpack in those three sentences. I started with the most obvious one.

"Was he murdered?" I asked.

"He was nineteen, and he died because he hit his head. The police thought he tripped and kiboshed himself on a table."

"But you don't," I said.

"None of fandom did," Ira said. "But most of us didn't know nothing. I didn't even hear he was dead for two weeks after."

I nodded. I felt a little chilled. I had no idea that anyone had been murdered in fandom. I didn't think of us as a particularly violent bunch. Even the Great Worldcon War never really came to blows. Ira and Sam agreed on that at least.

Murder. It happened in our community like every other community, although not at cons. Like Barbara, who ran a comic book store in Michigan. She was murdered just a few years before this conversation, and later (much later) her husband was convicted, and it all became fodder for a *Dateline* episode a few years back, because of the SF/comic connection.

The mention of an old homicide, though, got me thinking like the detective I'm supposed to be.

I asked, "When you introduced the new slides, did you

mention that they were part of a group of slides you just found or did you not mention that at all?"

"I didn't say I found them," Ira said stiffly. "I said my son happened upon them. An entire box. A big box."

I shifted slightly, wishing I could stand without being rude.

"And you said there'd be more in future presentations?" I asked.

"Yes, Spade. That's just good marketing. You know that."

"Are the photos protected now?" I asked.

"Protected?" Ira's voice went up. "Protected? What do you mean, Spade?"

I didn't mean to upset him further, that was for certain. But I was. Still, I needed answers to these questions.

"Where are they?" I asked with trepidation. "At your house?"

"No," he said, and shook his head for emphasis. "I gave them to my son. He's having them all converted to slides at my request."

"This is David, right?" I asked. Ira had three sons and a daughter. I had just been assuming that the son who had the pictures was the son who lived in Manhattan.

"Yes, David. Everyone else left New York." Ira said that as if he couldn't believe anyone would make that choice ever.

I let out a small breath.

"Why?" Ira asked.

"Noodling," I said. "The other slides, they have photographic backup too, right?"

Ira's lower lip started trembling again. "No. I thought you knew that. My wife made me keep them in a storage unit and it got flooded in the 1970s. Negatives, everything. Gone."

By the end of that speech, his voice was trembling too. That was what disturbed him about the loss of the slides.

He couldn't replace them.

He leaned forward and grabbed my hands, startling me.

"They're all I have of those years," he said. "All I have of those friends. It's how I..."

He shook his head, and that movement shook a tear loose.

"I understand," I said, and I thought I did. I do understand more now, as I'm writing this, even though I'm still not even close to eighty-five. But Ira is gone now, as are so many others of my friends, and all I have of them are memories that no one else shares.

I couldn't—and can't—imagine the weight that a gregarious eighty-five-year-old felt when faced with continual losses spread over decades.

"I'll find them," I promised. Stupidly. Real-life detectives, police officers, and others—they never make promises like that.

But I did.

Ira squeezed my hands again.

"It's okay, Spade," he said. "My son, David, he tells me I gotta let the memories go. I can't keep everything that reminds me of something."

He choked on the last few words. Then he swallowed and continued.

"I'm trying, Spade. I really am." He gave me a watery smile. "Getting old. It ain't no picnic."

"I know," I said. I was sincere, even though, in hindsight, I didn't know at all.

———

Okay, I'm ashamed of this next part, but I'm going to tell it anyway.

After I managed to get Ira to head downstairs to join the sweet young fan for a belated brunch, I went to Con Ops. That was where my Tower of Terror lived.

I brought some of my computers with me everywhere. They were large towers that held disks and data and had hard drives and all kinds of what were then more powerful than any locomotive that other desktops had. I always have state-of-the-art computer systems because of my Microsoft days, and back then, I ran everything in Con Ops from those Towers of Terror.

On a Sunday morning, Con Ops had an eerie resemblance to the *Marie Celeste*—the ghost ship that was discovered that looked like everyone had vanished midmeal. There were candy wrappers everywhere, open cans of Coke, Dr Pepper, and every other soft drink you could think of except the zero-calorie kind, as well as coffee cups scattered across every surface, except the one holding my computer.

The folks who ran conventions learned long ago that the only time I ever showed anything like wrath was if someone brought food or drink near the Towers of Terror. In that, I was the 1970s Lou Ferrigno Hulk, only without the body builder's muscles. Just the Bill Bixby catch phrase:

Don't make me angry. You wouldn't like me when I'm angry.

I was one of the first people ever to move my paper Rolodex onto my computer. And because I had a lot of confidential information from my days as a forensic accountant, I had the thing password protected at the NSA level.

But I also kept every phone number and piece of contact information I ever gathered, and that included the contact information for Ira's son David, acquired when we were planning a non-con dinner in Manhattan a dozen years before.

After I found the number, I wrote it on a piece of paper and took it up to my room. I didn't want anyone to overhear the conversation and have it get back to Ira. Even though Con Ops was empty that Sunday morning, I knew it probably wouldn't remain empty for long.

My suite was smaller than Ira's and not as tidy. After five days of almost no sleep (I generally arrive at cons I'm working at on Tuesday), I can't be expected to clean up past picking my underwear and dirty T-shirts off the floor.

Housekeeping hadn't arrived yet, so I sat on one of the flimsy chairs in front of the so-called desk that this room had and punched David's number into the hotel phone.

To my surprise, David answered on the second ring.

"Pops?" he asked.

"Um...no," I said. "It's Spade."

After I got the name out, I wasn't sure if he would remember who that even was.

"Oh, Dad's detective friend. It's been a long time." David's voice was wary. "I expected a call from Dad from this number."

Apparently, David had put the hotel's number into his Caller ID.

"He okay?" David asked, and that was when I twigged to the worry. David was afraid that something would happen to his father, alone at an SF convention.

"He's a little emotional," I said, "but otherwise all right."

David let out a sigh of relief. "So this is about...?"

I told him about the missing carousel. I also asked him not to tell his father that I had called.

"I'm looking into what happened," I said. "But before I conduct an actual investigation, I need to know something."

"What?" David sounded wary all over again.

"Your father," I said. "How's his memory?"

"*My* father?" David asked, sounding incredulous. "You're asking about *my* father?"

"Yes," I said. "He mentioned his moving out of his house and I was wondering if it was because, you know, of health issues?"

"You're asking if he has dementia." David laughed. "Seriously.

My father. No, Mr. Spade. He doesn't have dementia. He's the guy who remembers every time I farted at the dinner table from 1972 through the present."

I chuckled because I was supposed to.

"His memory is fine. The move is his idea. The house is too big for him, and I think something spooked him. He tripped or he dropped something or maybe he just realized that a house like that is a landmine for the unwary." The laughter had left David's voice. "He's moving into my building, but still will have his own place. With fewer traps for the unwary. The tough part is getting rid of all the family heirlooms. I made my siblings promise to take their fair share, even if they put the crap into storage. Otherwise Dad wouldn't have moved."

I understood that. I had no idea what would happen to my possessions after I no longer had use for them, but I wasn't willing to part with them—not yet, anyway.

"Thanks," I said. "I was concerned. Your father calls these memories, and I wasn't sure if his memories were stolen by a person or by time itself."

"Naw," David said. "My father's memory is as sharp as ever, maybe sharper. I wouldn't argue with him about anything, Mr. Spade. He has more room in that brain than anyone I've ever met."

I nodded, feeling embarrassed. I hadn't trusted my own instincts with Ira. I always thought he was a man who forgot nothing, but I let his age and one small detail about his life shake that perception.

But I did need to know whether or not he had gotten absent-minded. Or worse.

And now I did.

"Listen," David said before I could end the conversation,

"don't tell my dad but someone broke into the house this morning. That's why I don't want him to live there."

Now, he had my attention. "Did they take anything?"

"Naw," David said. "My dad has the nosiest neighbors this side of a *Bewitched* episode. Their version of Gladys Kravitz called the cops and they arrived within five minutes. Dad's not going to have that kind of service in Manhattan, let me tell you."

"Was someone arrested?" I asked.

"Stupid small borough cops," David said. "Arrived with sirens blaring and lights flashing. No, of course they didn't catch anyone. Not sure they wanted to."

I thanked him, frowning. Old detectives in books always said there were no coincidences, but you live long enough and you realize that there are a lot of coincidences.

Just not here. I was pretty sure that break-in and the loss of the carousel were tied together. I needed to find that carousel before whoever took it had a chance to destroy it and all the memories contained in those little 2" x 2" slides.

———

To start, I needed Doris's help. I hadn't worked much with the Escher Hotel on that year's Eschercon, so I had no contacts there. I needed to know something that I wasn't sure they could tell me.

I found her in the greenroom, settling an early morning fight between two Big Name panelists. Each wanted to moderate the ten a.m. panel and use it to force an agenda that the other disagreed with.

I didn't have time to wait for the eons' old fight to find some kind of momentary truce. Instead, I beckoned her, told her I thought that Ira's slides had been stolen, and asked her to go with me to the front desk.

She looked shocked and asked the $64,000 question: *Who would want to steal those slides?*

I told her I didn't know, even though that was half a lie. I had a small idea as to who might have stolen them, although that plus the break-in at Ira's house did take the theft to a level I hadn't expected.

Doris grabbed Carole B, who was making sure that the green-room snacks were being replaced (particularly the coffee) and assigned her the task of getting the Big Names to their panel.

Then Doris led me to the front desk, and asked for the manager. When she arrived, all official in her suit jacket, except for a tiny Superman pin that she must have gotten from Julius Schwartz, one of the most influential editors from the Silver Age of comics, who handed the pins out to anyone he liked or who had done him a favor. The pin endeared her to me. She could have just thanked him and put it in her desk.

"We had a theft in one of the rooms," Doris said quietly, even though no one was near the front desk at the moment.

Most of the fen had Monday checkout, so they could stick around for the Dead Dog Party. Those who didn't had late check-out, and hadn't even gotten up yet.

The manager looked disturbed and was about to ask a question, when Doris continued, "It was a targeted theft. Only one very precious item was taken."

I could see dollar signs flashing over the manager's head. *How much liability did the hotel have? What would this do to their reputation? What if the culprit was someone on staff?*

So I stepped in. "The item had value only to the person in the room. And obviously to the person who stole it. We're not talking about the Hope Diamond or anything."

To her credit, the manager's expression didn't change, although her shoulders visibly relaxed.

"What do you need from me?" she asked.

Doris looked at me. I'd thought for a while how to phrase this question.

I gave the manager Ira's room number and said, "I need to know who had a key to that room."

The manager immediately jumped on the computer and dug up the information. "It looks like the couple staying there have the only two keys."

She was referring to actual keys, not key cards. Back then, only the high-end hotels in the biggest of cities had them.

"Couple?" Doris said. "Do you have the right room?"

The manager repeated the number to her. "That's the room, right?"

I put a hand on Doris's arm, stopping her. "When did the wife pick up her key?"

The manager clacked a few keys. "Yesterday at five thirty."

Not long after Ira's presentation finished. And a half an hour after the group of us met for dinner. We'd been loud and laughing as we headed over to the most expensive restaurant in the Escher complex.

A lot of people would have noticed us.

"Did she leave her name, by chance?" I asked, knowing it was a long shot.

She thinned her lips. "Your questions are making me wonder what's awry here."

"Ira's a widower," Doris said.

"And he's not prone to taking other women into his room or to giving out his key," I said.

"Someone's going to get in trouble for this," the manager said.

"Don't," I said. "It's not your desk's fault."

"They should have checked identification," the manager said.

"And probably did," I said. "Many people in our community

don't share last names. I'll wager the woman who got the key was of an age with Ira, so your employee thought nothing of the request."

"You're being charitable," the manager said. "I think we should call the police."

"Not yet," I said. "What's been stolen has no physical value. So the police won't really pay attention."

The manager frowned at me.

"I would like to talk with the person on the desk last night, if I could," I said.

"He won't be in until two," the manager said.

I hoped to have everything wrapped up by then, but I didn't mention that. "Do you have a security system? Maybe a camera pointing at the desk?"

"We don't record," the manager said. "Privacy concerns."

I resisted the urge to look at Doris. I'd been telling her that the Escher Hotel was getting rough around the edges, but that comment confirmed it. Hotels usually didn't care about that kind of privacy unless they knew their hotel was being used for illegal hook-ups or other shady businesses.

We thanked the manager and left the desk. If my assumption was correct, my suspect pool was small.

"What do you want to do?" Doris asked me.

"I'm going to talk to a few people," I said, "and then I'll let you know."

The first person on my list was standing, bleary-eyed, at the coffee and pastry spread that this convention was famous for. So many fen didn't want much more than that for breakfast. They wanted to grab something quick and head to their panel.

I excused myself and walked over to the table. I grabbed a paper plate and covered it with a cherry Danish.

"Ava," I said to the woman next to me. "Can I have a minute?"

She blinked at me. "Oh, the pretend detective man," she said.

I made myself smile. "That's me."

"For the record," she said. "I didn't do it. I claim credit for all of my crimes and I haven't committed one since I got here."

"Good to know," I said. "But I don't want to talk to you about crimes."

"Oh?" she asked.

I could see Doris out of the corner of my eye. She looked surprised too.

"Let's just grab a seat," I said, waving a hand at one of the seating groups at the far side of the lobby.

"You got fifteen minutes, Big Boy," Ava said, and picked up a coffee to go with her plate full of croissants. I took a water. I'd get something caffeinated later.

We walked across the lobby to the pleather chairs. No one was sitting there, although a few more fen were emerging from the nearby elevators, looking as bleary as Ava had.

"I wanted to talk to you about Ira's presentation," I said.

"You don't get to yell at me, kid," she said. "Ira's been passing off his memories as the truth for years now."

"I'm not going to yell," I said. "I want to know about the new slides. You said he got a few things wrong."

I didn't add that it bothered Ira, because she already knew that. Besides, I wanted the focus to be on the slides, not on Ira.

"Oh," she said, "he's been doing it for years."

"What's that?" I asked.

"Confusing Fred Pohl with Mervin DeGrastene." She took a bite from a croissant and immediately pastry flakes covered her gray *I'm old, not stupid* sweatshirt.

"Why does that bother you?" I asked.

She frowned at me, then leaned back. Those eyes were sharp. "Does this have anything to do with Ira's sad face this morning?"

"Very good deflection," I said, hoping I could deflect as well. "Please, just answer the question."

She looked down, saw the pastry flakes, and wiped them off the front of her sweatshirt. I got the sense that she didn't want me to see her reaction.

"Look, kid," she said, "details matter. It matters that he confuses them."

"Why?" I asked. I almost said, *They're his memories, after all*, but that would make this about Ira. I had a sense it was something more.

She sighed. "You're not gonna let this go, are you?"

"No," I said.

She looked up, and all pretense was gone from her face. I saw a tired woman who, in her own way, looked as sad as Ira did.

"No one remembers Mervin, not really, and I'm not sure they should."

"Then why did you bring it up?" I asked.

"Because his pictures need to be excised from all writings about fandom," she said with such viciousness that I almost leaned back.

"Why?" I asked.

"Oh, just ask any other woman who was around then," she said and started to stand.

I reached out and almost grabbed her arm, then decided that was a bad idea. "Please," I said. "I'll work with Ira, if you just tell me what's going on."

"You know Mervin was killed, right?" Ava said as she sank back into the chair.

"I just found out this morning. I heard it was an accident."

"Accident schmaccident," Ava said. "In my day, someone'd call that justifiable homicide."

I stiffened. "What happened?"

"I honestly don't know for sure," Ava said. "But I do know cops investigated and talked to half of the women in fandom at the time. Which was probably three of us."

She let out a bitter laugh.

I waited, because what else could I do?

"He did the same with all of us," she said. "We don't talk about it. I didn't go near men for a long time after that, not that anyone noticed or cared. And then the war, and there were other things..."

Her voice trailed off. But her eyes remained defiant.

"You know, Ira always thought I pushed him away because of him. In those days, Mr. Pretend Detective, women didn't talk to anyone but other women about men like Mervin. We warned each other to stay away."

She still wasn't saying exactly what happened, although I could guess.

"He hurt you," I said, deciding to be as elliptical as I could.

"Oh, hell, no," she said. "Hurt is not the word you young people use. He took what he wanted and I couldn't fight hard enough. Clear enough for you?"

My cheeks were flushed. I wasn't going to use the word *rape* if she wasn't. I didn't want to shut her down.

"Clear," I said.

"And there was one of us," Ava said. "I know she went to Mervin's apartment that day, voluntarily, because I couldn't talk her out of it. I also know she was a mess for years, and I know that she once asked my husband—a career prosecutor in the City—if you shoved someone and they died, was that a homicide?"

"What was his response?" I asked.

She glared at me. "I loved my husband, but he wasn't the most sensitive man in the history of the universe. He said, depends on the circumstances, but unless you called the police and reported it right away, it would probably be considered manslaughter at best."

I let out a small breath. Manslaughter. "Do I know this person?" I asked.

"Yeah," she said. "And it isn't me, if you were wondering. But that's all you'll get out of me."

I nodded as if that was okay, which, on some level, it was.

"The photos, what did they show?" I asked.

"Have Ira show you," she said.

"I can't," I said. "Someone stole the carousel."

I didn't tell her that the same someone had a friend or friends break into his house to find other pictures.

"Oh, for Pete's sake," she said, then let out a sigh. "The photos weren't of Fred and his latest patootie, which is what Ira said. I pulled him aside later, said he was disrespecting Leslie—"

Leslie Perri, Fred's first wife, whom he met in fandom around that time, and who had died long before I entered fandom.

"—and he needed to cut it out. Fred always had women, but he was faithful when he was married." Ava sighed. "Ira's just jealous. Fred could attract women by doing nothing. Ira had to work at it. And before you ask, I was not one of Fred's 'patooties.' God, I hate that word. But Fred and me, we still don't get along much."

"Yet you're defending him," I said.

"I'm not," she said. "He just shouldn't be confused with that piece of filth Mervin."

"So who was the woman he was with?" I asked.

"C'mon, Mr. Pretend Detective," she said. "Two plus two shouldn't be that hard for someone like you, especially since she got scared and actually stole the evidence."

"Evidence of what?" I asked.

"Unless I miss my guess," Ava said, "that photo was the last one taken of Mervin alive."

———

In all my years investigating small crimes at SF conventions, I'd never had a fictional detective moment before—y'know, where the pieces fell into place so quickly that a chill ran down my back. I'd also never dealt with an actual death before, even if it happened years before I was born.

Ava was right. Two plus two wasn't hard. And she was wrong about one thing. There were more than six women in those early years of SF, although not all were members of First Fandom or even came back to fandom after the war.

But Evelyn Chastain had. In Ira's photos, she looked like a tiny bird with great taste in clothes, always wearing a dress with a flare skirt and low heels that made her look like a 1930s movie star, until the camera caught her face and couldn't get past the thick glasses to reveal her eyes.

Evelyn still wore thick glasses, but on a birdlike elderly woman they looked appropriate.

I found her in the hallway outside a panel on the roots of modern science fiction.

"May we talk?" I asked.

She hobbled toward me, her walker barely keeping her upright. At least it was the proper height. She was maybe five feet tall these days and so thin it looked like she could disappear if she turned sideways.

"You haven't destroyed Ira's carousel yet, have you?" I asked.

She looked at me sharply, and nearly lost her balance. "How'd you know?"

I could've told her about the things I'd discovered, but I didn't. I also knew she had the means and the wherewithal to hire someone to break into Ira's house and take that box.

"I talked to the front desk," I said. "They believed that Ira's wife asked for an extra key. The young man at the desk would've believed that only a few people here were married to Ira."

She let out a sad laugh. "Age wins again," she said.

"Did you destroy it?" I asked.

"No," she said. "Not that it matters."

"It matters to Ira," I said. "His memories are in there."

She leaned one arm on the walker and tapped her forehead with the other. "His memories are in there."

I shook my head. "Ira's a little different than most people. He likes to see his memories in black and white."

Her mouth thinned, but she didn't say anything.

"If I get Ira to promise not to show any pictures of Mervin DeGrastene," I said, "will you return the carousel?"

"Ira confuses Mervin and Fred," she said quietly.

"I know," I said. "You have no problems with the old slides. Just the new ones, right?"

She raised her tiny chin. "You know why," she said with a touch of incredulity.

"I know nothing," I said. "Except that as far as the police are concerned, Mervin's death was labeled an accident, and there's no open case file."

"And that matters how?" she asked.

I wasn't a lawyer. I'm still not. But I do think about justice sometimes.

"As I see it," I said, "there's four potential crimes here. One attempted but thwarted, one that would've been charged the way a prosecutor told you years ago and a modern jury would've considered self-defense. Then there's a minor theft of valueless Kodak Carousel, and a more serious break-in at an elderly man's abode."

Her eyes narrowed. The movement seemed larger than it was, thanks to her thick lenses.

"It seems to me," I said, "that the only one today's police would care about is the break-in. Then they'd want to know why, and they'd start digging in places that don't need any investigation at all."

"Is that a threat?" she asked, her voice wobbling just a little.

I hunched, trying to make myself less threatening.

"No." I made my voice as gentle as possible. "I suspect whatever happened—"

"It was self-defense!" she said so loudly that all five people in the corridor (two Klingons, a hotel employee, and two not-yet-famous writers) looked at us.

"I know," I said, and let the words hang.

She stepped closer to her walker, as if she felt wobbly, but I knew better than to touch her.

"I'm not going to say anything," I said. "And other people, who've suspected for years, haven't said anything either."

"Then how do you know?" she asked.

"I pulled it out of the wife of that prosecutor who scared the crap out of you," I said.

Evelyn smiled at me. "You think you can get me to confess."

"To the carousel, yes," I said. "The rest of it, there's nothing to confess."

She looked down at her walker, then said, "You know, Ira and I don't agree about much. He thinks the history is so danged good. He thinks we were all so happy. None of us were happy. That's why we banded together. We needed something else to talk about besides having no money and what was going on in Europe."

I waited.

Then she looked up at me and shrugged. "I should never have gone to his presentation."

I nodded.

She squared her thin shoulders. "If I give him back the carousel, can you make sure he doesn't use the slides of Mervin? That bastard doesn't deserve to be mentioned as part of fandom."

"I think I can do that," I said.

"*Without* telling Ira what happened," she said.

That would be harder, but I had a hunch I could do it.

"Yes," I said.

"I don't want to talk to Ira," she said.

"You don't have to," I said. "You still have his key, right?"

"Yes," she said.

"Let's just put the carousel back in his room."

———

Which was what we did. I had to tell Ira that I dealt with the culprit, so that he wouldn't worry that he had somehow missed seeing the carousel. I didn't want him to suddenly be concerned about his own mental health.

Then I lied to him. I told him that Fred still didn't like being confused with Mervin and it would be better for all if any Fred or Mervin pictures weren't in the presentation.

"I can do that," Ira said so quickly that I realized that the history between him and Fred was as touchy as I thought it might have been.

At future cons, Ira used new slides, but kept his promise. And he also kept his carousel locked up in the hotel safe at night.

He never asked me who took the carousel. He was just happy to get it back. I'm not sure if Ava told him. I know Evelyn didn't. Until the end of her days, she remained true to her word. She never showed up at one of his presentations again.

They changed, those presentations, particularly after more and more of the original members of First Fandom passed. Ira removed the slides that used to anger Sam after Sam died. Ira added a few gorgeous slides of Ava after her death—loving shots that I think he never ever showed her.

A few weeks ago, Ira died. His son David called me and offered me the entire slide show.

"I thought your dad was giving it to the Science Fiction Museum," I said.

"They want someone to go through it," David said. "I don't have the heart or the knowledge."

So Ira's slides—Ira's memories—are spread out over my kitchen table. I'm going to digitize them to preserve all of them.

But I keep staring at one of a birdlike woman who was no one's patootie next to a man who bore a slight resemblance to the young Fred Pohl. Only that man had ice-cold eyes, and hands the size of meat hammers.

I like to think I would have seen Mervin DeGrastene for what he was if I ever met him, but I'm not sure any of us ever see others for who they are.

The histories that Ira knew and conveniently forgot, the undercurrents among a group of young adults who had no idea what kind of hell their generation was about to face, are lost now. Some of the faces in these shots I don't recognize, and the people who could've identified them are gone too.

There are candid shots that aren't going to the museum and some photographs that'll never see the light of day because of my conversations with Evelyn and Ava.

Ira left me his memories so that I could sort them, and make sure they didn't hurt anyone. Ira had cleansed them, made them harmless, made his friends harmless, and took all the complexities out of their young lives. The good, the bad, and some of the ugly.

Stories. That's what he trafficked in. That's what he turned his memories into. Stories that comforted him and pretended that everything was right for a brief shining moment in the world before it spiraled into a nightmare.

Because for him, that's what the moment was. Even with the Great Worldcon War, that he ignored. The Exclusion Act, the split in his beloved fandom, the fact that most of these kids continued their fight long after it ceased to matter.

It was small. It was easy to focus on. It allowed them to ignore the pain of life midcentury.

I get that now, and I want to talk to him about it.

But of course, I can't.

THE CASE OF THE PURLOINED PAGES
A SPADE/PALADIN CONUNDRUM

1

Paladin snapped her fingers in front of my face.

"Spade," she said, snapping again. "Earth to Spade."

We were sitting in a deli about a half a block down from the stupidly expensive Times Square hotel we were staying in. The deli's décor had too much orange for my taste. Across from me was some artist's renderings of Ebbets Field, where the Brooklyn Dodgers played, a long, long time ago. At some point, New York was going to have to get over the fact that the Dodgers left Brooklyn before most of us were born.

She slammed a flat palm on the table, making my smoked salmon Benedict and side order of bagel with cream cheese jump. I didn't jump.

I looked at her slowly. She knew better than to snap her fingers at me or slap a hand on the table to get my attention. I have very few rules about anything, but those gestures strike me as rude, and I've let her—and most of my friends—know that I'm not fond of them.

"I'm right here, Paladin," I said.

"It doesn't seem like it," she said, grabbing her fork. She had ordered a pastrami omelet with an extra egg, and layered with Swiss cheese. She eats like that a lot, and I have no idea where she puts it all.

Paladin is tiny, with short-cropped brown hair and ears that are naturally pointed. Half of science fiction fandom is fascinated by her ears, but woe to the person who tries to touch one to see if they're real. I've seen her grab the offender with one hand, twist his arm around his back, and bring him to his knees, whimpering in pain, in less than a second.

"Sorry," I said. I tucked into my breakfast as well. Ugly as this deli was, its food was spectacular, which was more than I could say for the snotty hotel we had booked at the last minute.

That place didn't even have a breakfast café. We could eat at Starbucks if we wanted to sink that low, or get boxed food for our room. Nothing opened in the hotel until three when the high-end restaurants and their high-end bars threw the doors open and expected us to pay $45 for a mediocre corned beef sandwich. (I know; I picked one up shortly after I arrived, starving and running late from the airport.)

"You see someone you recognize?" she asked.

I saw a lot of people I recognized, all of them mystery writers who had come to this particular part of Manhattan to go to the Edgar Awards on Thursday. Despite all of the changes in publishing the past several years, the Edgars managed to hang onto their prestige.

Presented by the Mystery Writers of America, the awards covered the gamut from best novel to best short story and back again. None of these came out of a popular vote; they were judged by a panel of their peers.

Sometimes the Edgars missed the best books of the year, but often they had their fingers on the pulse. A lot of the winners over its decades-spanning history managed to remain not only relevant but incredibly great reads.

I usually don't come to the Edgars, though. It's a schmooze-fest filled with everyone who is anyone (remaining) in New York publishing. People come to be seen. The nominees—many of whom have never been to the festivities—walk around looking as if they've been hit on the head with a piano. Either they're stunned at the writerly (and actual) celebrity around them or they're honored just to be nominated.

The ceremony itself is short on assholes and idiots, unlike ceremonies held at most science fiction conventions, which is usually where I go for ceremony. I've helped with too many Hugo Award ceremonies to be gosh-wowed by anything that happened there. I always avoid the Nebulas and World Fantasy Awards, because they're just not relevant to my little corner of sf fandom, and I still haven't decided if I like the Dragon Award ceremonies or not.

But then, I usually don't have a dog in the hunt—not even a favorite book. The stuff I read doesn't get nominated in sf for political reasons, and I don't like ranking fiction anyway. It's a matter of taste.

My mystery tastes don't run to fiction. I do enough work in the crime field (often reluctantly) to find most of the mysteries that I read a bit contrived, although Paladin—who has an unexpected taste for golden age mysteries as well as hardboiled novels of all persuasions—thinks that even the crimes we have investigated over our strange partnership are contrived as well.

"I don't see anyone important," I said in answer to Paladin's question. Actually, I did see a lot of important mystery writers, who would hate to be characterized as unimportant, but I wasn't really referring to that kind of important.

No one important to *us*. Me and Paladin.

"I can't imagine you're interested in Ebbets Field," she said, looking at the mural. "So what gives? I thought we were having a conversation."

What gives. I'd never heard that phrase from her before. It was both old-fashioned, and quite New York.

I made myself look at her. Her blue eyes were snapping. She was getting impatient.

"I was thinking about the numbers you gave me," I said.

"I didn't *give* you numbers," she said. "I gave you papers. A lot of them."

With numbers on them, but I wasn't going to say that. No sense correcting her.

"You already told me," she said, her voice lower than it had been a minute ago. "They don't make sense."

"They don't make sense in an odd way." I am a forensic accountant, among many other things. But my forensic accountant work usually brings me to court for businesses and other legal problems.

Generally, though, Paladin and I work cases at science fiction conventions, things one or the other of us stumble upon. We have dealt with attacks on fen (the word for a group of fans), and we've dealt with a potential bombing. We've handled cases that involved missing teenagers, and we rescued one of them, who is now—to use an old-fashioned term—our ward.

Not that Paladin and I are an item; we're not, no matter how much I might want it. (Not that I would act on it *ever*. I wouldn't want to do anything to jeopardize our friendship.) We just pool our resources to take care of Casper, who is probably one of the smartest people I know. She's currently in a boarding school in

San Francisco, a school for other incredibly smart people, and she's blowing them all out of the water.

"What kind of odd way?" Paladin asked.

"That's what I can't explain." I pushed at the salmon, which looked just as orange as the walls. "I can't put my finger on it."

"Maybe you should get back to your computers before we go," she said.

We were supposed to meet Paladin's client. Paladin had been really cagey about all of this—who the client was, why we had to see said client in person, and where the numbers came from.

I could see the papers in my mind. I have an eidetic memory, particularly for numbers. The numbers looked okay on the surface; they were lists of payments and expenses, along with some income, albeit not much.

The expenses were low for any city in America at the moment. They included rent, and the client—according to Paladin—lived in a rent-controlled apartment on the Upper West Side. That had to piss someone off. I knew that a number of the apartment buildings had gone condo in the past two decades, and some of the buyouts were stalled by people who had lived in a rent-controlled environment for most of their lives.

But those numbers didn't look right to me either, and I couldn't do due diligence, because Paladin wasn't giving me the details I needed, like the name of the client and the client's exact address.

Then there was the gathering here in New York. She insisted on coming to the Edgars, and she wanted to stay in the official hotel.

I asked point-blank if the client was one of the nominees. She had laughed and said, *Not on your life.*

Here's the weird thing. *I* get clients, mostly for my non-sf-related work. Paladin gets cases. Usually emergency ones—some kid goes missing, or some pervert has threatened someone Paladin knows. Paladin usually takes care of the perverts herself, in a manner that I'd prefer not to know about.

She finds the missing kids and gets them assistance, often without me, but sometimes, I get to pull strings. I know a lot of people, both in and out of fandom. The ones in fandom prove the most useful, because sf fandom has secret pockets—people whose real lives are important, but their relaxation is cosplay or gaming or *Star Trek*. Geekery means a lot to folk.

It means a lot to me, even though it's changing. I find it odd that geekery has become a lot more accepted in recent years, enough so that I'm no longer apologizing for the nerdy references that slip out when I'm talking to real-world clients.

"I wish you'd stop being so mysterious," I said to Paladin, finally letting my irritation out. "I could probably figure out what's going on with these numbers if I had all the facts before me."

Her tiny bow-shaped mouth thinned, a warning side that Paladin was getting irritated too.

"I promised the client I'd bring you and they could vet you. They're jumpy, and I'm beginning to think for good reason."

Then she sat up, and frowned at one of the round shoplifting mirrors perched in a corner. She could see who had entered the diner and who was leaving. She had pointed the mirrors out to me when we arrived, because I had commented on how strange it was that Paladin was sitting with her back to the door.

Apparently, she felt safe with the mirrors in place.

I sat a little taller, but didn't see anyone unusual. Just more mystery writers, threading their way in, talking loudly, and demanding a seat. This group was notable only for the preponderance of bestsellers—three that I could easily see.

But that wasn't unusual. The bestsellers loved to come to New

York, they loved to hang out at both the Edgars and the Thriller Writers' banquets because they could get attention for their work without being bombarded by adoring fans.

Some writers—George R. R. Martin comes to mind—remember their own humble beginnings as a reader and a fan and a baby writer, and attend as many conventions as will have them, provided the con can provide for their safety.

But the majority of writers, particularly those with a lot of name recognition, prefer to pretend that their readers don't matter, and that signing autographs is a chore rather than a duty.

There were at least two in the chore/duty group clustered near the door, folks I rarely spoke to because they didn't want to deal with me. I guess I'd pointed out too many times that they were nothing without their readers.

I looked back at Paladin, who was stirring her omelet into a pile of mush, a sign that she was done eating.

"What's going on?" I asked.

She glanced at the mirror.

I looked too, saw that the latest group of mystery writers were being led into a side room, so that they could be boisterous in semi-privacy. She relaxed just a little.

"Let's finish up," she said and slid slightly backward in the booth so that she could reach inside the right front pocket of her jeans.

"I got it," I said, waving at the nonexistent check. From what I could tell, Paladin did fine with her finances, but I'm one of the few Microsoft Millionaires who managed to hang onto his money and turn it into more millions. A breakfast at a New York diner wasn't going to break me.

To my surprise, she didn't even argue. She slipped out of the booth, grabbed a piece of toast, and said, "I'll get us a taxi," and headed to the door before I could stop her.

It wasn't raining, so it probably wouldn't be hard to get a cab, which meant I was on some kind of clock. I managed to flag our server, wend my way through the much-too-complex digital paying system (which wanted my damn opinion about everything from service to bagels), and got to the main door just as another wave of mystery writers was heading in.

This group was friendlier. I recognized at least two of the women from science fiction conventions. Everyone wanted to talk, but I had to slide my way past with a *Got a cab waiting*, and hoped they would understand.

Not that I slid well. I took up half the door as I went through, nearly careening into an agent that I'd tangled with when, for my sins, I'd stepped in to run programming at a Readercon.

She glared at me, I glared at her, and when she wouldn't move out of my way, I bowed and extravagantly swept my hand to the door.

"Milady," I said.

"Jerk," she replied and went inside.

Paladin was standing on the curb next to a yellow cab that was idling with its available light off. She had the back door open, and she was shifting from foot to foot. More than once as I made my way across the sidewalk, she had to fend off people—all men—who wanted to join her in that cab.

When I reached her side, one of the men raised his eyebrows at me as if he couldn't believe I would be with a woman that petite and pretty. Paladin's looks were deceptive, which was one of her superpowers.

I grinned at him, and grabbed the door frame from Paladin. She went around the cab rather than sliding through, and let herself in on the driver's side.

I climbed into the passenger side. At least ancient New York cabs had more legroom than most modern conveyances, which almost makes up for the smell of stale sweat, the fingerprint-covered plastic partition, and the unknown substance in the cracks on the bench seat.

Paladin settled in, and as I pulled the door closed, the cab jutted forward into traffic as if we were being chased by a supervillain. I slammed against the back of the seat, and groped for some kind of seatbelt. After a moment, I found it, realized it was never going to accommodate me, and let it fall to the seat.

At that same moment, I realized that Paladin had already given the cab the address, which irritated me all over again. I didn't like how secretive she was being.

The cab made an illegal U-turn half a block from the hotel, then headed uptown at a rate of speed that made me grip the armrest on the door. We dodged bike messengers, motorcyclists, and idiots on motorized skateboards that somehow seemed to find their way into the middle of traffic.

My breakfast was churning in my stomach, which irritated me as well. That breakfast had been the highlight of my morning; I didn't really want to revisit it because of a cab driver with a death wish.

We stopped outside the Dakota, of all places, probably one of the most famous apartment buildings in all of New York City. Instantly, my antennae went up. Something was off in either the facts that Paladin gave me or with those numbers. Or maybe we were going to walk to another building.

Paladin leaned forward to pay the cabbie, long before I could even grab my wallet, and then she ducked out of the cab as if someone had lit it on fire. She stopped in front of the building.

Nope. We weren't going anywhere else. This was our destination.

My heart pounded. Something was *weird*.

The Dakota was exclusive. Famous people lived there. Even

more famous people had their applications to live there denied by a notoriously picky co-op board that had fended off more than one suit about possible racism.

John Lennon was murdered just outside the apartment gates as he arrived home one December night. Fans of his still left flowers and came to the building on a pilgrimage.

I got out a bit more slowly than Paladin had, looking up at the graceful old building. Once upon a time, it had been the tallest building in this part of the city. Other buildings dwarfed it now, but it somehow managed to keep itself the center of attention.

It looked like a fortress, its brown façade well-maintained, and covered with all kinds of interest, from gables to dormers to finials. I could have spent hours just staring up at it—trying to ignore the incongruous air conditioning units that stuck out of the top of some of the windows, still.

I'd never been inside this place—not officially, anyway, although I'd seen countless images of it, from the movies to television. I hadn't expected how tall the south entry was, nor the gate that crossed it, or the flowering pots that stood on top of gigantic vases on either side of the expansive entry.

I admit it: I was gaping. Paladin punched my arm and pointed forward. Two doormen stood near the gate. Between them, a sign that read: *Authorized Persons Only Beyond This Point*.

Paladin led us up to one of the doormen, who gave her one of the most condescending looks I'd ever seen, even though he was the one in costume. A blue uniform with gold piping, a hat with a bill that read "The Dakota" on top, and a subtle little nametag that I couldn't read from this distance.

He would have looked dapper if it weren't for the fact that his black bow tie was crooked and his white shirt had lost its crispness hours ago.

"We're expected," Paladin said, handing him a piece of paper that she seemed to have pulled out of nowhere.

"This way, madam," he said, and let us through the wrought iron gate. We walked down the driveway into the famous interior courtyard, filled with spring flowers. The interior looked bigger and more imposing than I expected. Even though other buildings towered around the Dakota these days, you couldn't see them from inside this not-so-little haven.

The doorman led us past some azaleas and some red flowers I couldn't identify. The dominant smell, though, was lilies of the valley, which were clustered near some ornamental trees. I'd never seen quite so many lilies of the valley in any garden, but I didn't say anything.

Paladin looked grim as we walked past all the decorative beauty, as if it offended her somehow. I tried to take in everything, knowing I probably wouldn't ever come here again.

The doorman led us to one of the building's four corners. Each one had an entry, and it only took me a few minutes to realize the Dakota was divided into quadrants, rather than having a single front door.

We went inside the nearest entrance, taking us into some kind of anteroom, which was darker than I expected. The wood paneling was so dark that not even the marble wainscoting could lighten it.

"The family would like you to take the stairs," the doorman said to Paladin, then stepped back to reveal what must have passed for a grand staircase when the building had been built in 1884. Staircases then weren't hidden.

I looked longingly at the elevator, but no one else seemed to notice. Paladin took the stairs two at a time. I gripped the wooden banister and climbed, feeling the sag of years on the stairs beneath my feet. I hoped she knew where she was going, because I wasn't going to make it more than two or three flights. Not without stopping on some landing somewhere and gasping for an embarrassing amount of time.

We rounded a corner. A light filtered down the stairs and as I reached the first floor, I realized that light came from an open door.

A woman stood in the doorway, leaning against a huge mahogany door. She was small, with pinched features and scared eyes. Her brown hair looked like it hadn't been properly trimmed in months, maybe years. I'd seen a lot of fen who took scissors to their own hair whose ends were less ragged than hers.

She wore a baggy sweatshirt, and some loose green pants over a pair of scuffed sneakers. When she saw Paladin, she smiled enough to soften her face.

"I'm Louise," she said. "Thanks for coming."

Paladin nodded. "This is the friend I told you about," and she moved a hand to indicate me.

"Yes, I checked up on you." Louise made it sound like she was looking for criminal activity. "I'm told you prefer to be called Mr. Spade?"

I was surprised. I thought we had come so that the client—apparently this Louise woman—could vet me.

"Spade is fine," I said.

She pushed the door back even farther so that we could walk through. I had no trouble getting inside. The edges were wide and the door itself had to be at least twelve feet high.

We stepped into a vestibule with a cut-glass chandelier over a faded blue rug. I couldn't tell if the rug had once had value or not. The straight-back chairs on either side of the door looked like they'd been in place forever and never used.

There was an umbrella stand near a table that had a bronze dish for keys as well as an open *New York Times* on its surface. I glanced at the headlines and saw that it was, indeed, today's paper.

"My aunt doesn't know you're here," Louise said. "I'd prefer to keep it that way. I'd like to go to the kitchen."

The idea that the niece didn't want us to see the aunt made me uncomfortable. Family dynamics were often odd and negotiating those was sometimes more difficult than solving whatever the problem was.

Paladin didn't seem upset, though. I'd wait and see what was going to happen, so I let Paladin lead.

We turned left from the entry, past a living room that had curtains closed to the street so that I couldn't see much past the ghosts of some furniture.

We passed another room—dining, maybe?—and went through some interior doors that separated the working part of the apartment from the living spaces. I caught a whiff of some kind of medicinal smell.

But that faded as we went through one of the interior doors into a kitchen that hadn't been upgraded since the 1970s. The green-and-gold appliances told me that much, and the granite countertops made the room seem even darker than the mahogany cabinets did.

A Formica table sat underneath the room's single window, which overlooked the courtyard below. We were low enough to the ground to see the faces of people in the courtyard—not that there were many people walking about at this time of day.

"Can I get you anything?" Louise asked. "Coffee or something?"

"We just finished breakfast," Paladin said, but I added—because it was true—"I wouldn't mind some water."

Louise opened one of the large cabinets and removed a green water glass that had bubbles on the sides. I hadn't seen one of those since I was a kid. They weren't collectible, so far as I knew. She opened the refrigerator and removed one of the high-end water pitchers with its own filter. Before she poured, she asked, "Ice?"

"No thank you," I said. I didn't see an icemaker in the refrigerator's door—did those even exist in the 1970s?—and didn't want Louise to root around for some ice.

She handed me the glass, from which I drank a little more gratefully than I expected to. Paladin watched me, a tiny frown creasing her brow. She knew I was putting pieces together, but she clearly wasn't sure what pieces I was assembling.

When I finished drinking a little more than was seemly, I set the glass down.

"So," I asked in the most conversational tone I could muster, "how long has this apartment been in the family?"

Louise's eyebrows went up. She pulled out one of the chairs and sat down heavily. "What makes you ask that question?"

A lot of things that I wasn't going to share, the primary one being the numbers that Paladin had given me. Some of them were finally sliding into place.

"The décor, mostly," I said, not quite lying. "It's clearly an integral part of the apartment."

"Not everyone redoes their kitchens right away," Louise said a bit defensively. And she was right, but someone who had the millions it took to buy a place like this meant that any buyer would immediately gut the kitchen and put in modern appliances, even if those appliances looked retro.

Not that the 1970s was the appropriate retro for a building that was finished in the late nineteenth century.

I waited.

Louise glanced at Paladin, who tilted her head and said in a voice I'd only heard her use with children and traumatized teenagers, "You can trust him. That's why I brought him. He can figure this all out."

So that was the kind of vetting we were doing. Louise had to see for herself that she could trust me.

Apparently she decided she could because she said, " My family, they lived here since the building was built, and they were among the first to buy their unit when the building went co-op in the early 1960s."

"So the apartment is fully paid for," I said, rubbing my fingers over the ancient green water glass. I didn't look at Paladin. I didn't want to see her surprise.

She had told me that the client lived in a rent-controlled apartment, not that the client *owned* the apartment. That fact alone made a great deal of difference in every single one of the numbers that Paladin had given me.

"Yes." Louise almost sounded annoyed. "My family paid in full when they bought it."

"And no second mortgages?" I asked. Or third mortgages or fourth.

"No," Louise said. "Although my aunt has received offers for millions and millions over the years. She never wanted to sell."

"This is her place, then," I said.

Louise nodded. "It was going to go into a family trust, but that got stalled because the lawyers can't figure out the money."

She glanced at Paladin. I did too, finally. Paladin's expression was flat. I recognized it. She was annoyed. She must have felt like the client lied to her.

Louise continued, "The lawyers say nothing makes sense."

She got that in one. I made myself look away from Paladin. I didn't want her annoyance to become mine.

"But the ownership should be simple," I said. Provided Louise was telling me the truth and there were no other liens on the place.

"The ownership *is* simple," Louise said. "My brothers and I, we inherit if something happens to my aunt. But she wanted the apartment, and her work in a trust, so we don't have to pay taxes we can't afford, but the lawyers say there's something hinky about her finances and they won't finish the work until she clears it up. She's refusing."

Inheritance. Family disputes. The very things I avoid—outside of fandom, anyway, because fandom is often about family disputes as well.

"She's refusing?" I asked. "Is she ill? Is that why all of this is coming up? Is she even able to make decisions for herself right now?"

"I knew it would be like this," Louise said with a hint of anger. "Yes, of course she can make decisions for herself. I suppose you want to talk with her."

That was an interesting about-face. Was it because Louise had met me? Or because I had figured out the ownership of the apartment so quickly? That part wasn't hard, but I didn't say that to either of them.

"Yes, I would like to talk with her," I said.

Paladin watched me, letting me take the lead. Louise didn't seem to notice.

"Let me check with my aunt," Louise said. "She's so secretive. She didn't want me to bring in anyone, but the lawyers did, and she really doesn't want to leave this place to us without taking care of the taxes. We're at a standstill on this. She seems to think..."

Louise cut herself off, then shook her head. She opened her hands in one of those gestures people used when they believed they were trapped by a situation.

"I thought maybe bringing in someone who is not a regular detective or recommended by the lawyers might help," Louise said. "A friend of mine—you worked for her." That last was directed at Paladin. Paladin nodded, that blank expression still on her face. "My friend said you'd be good. Then you mentioned *him*."

She looked at me, eyes narrowing.

"You're not a regular detective," she said to Paladin, "but *he* is, isn't he?"

"You knew that," I said. "You said you investigated me."

"I figured you could help with the numbers," Louise said. "But now, you want to talk with my aunt."

"I do," I said, sensing her reluctance. "I can sign any kind of nondisclosure you want. I even have a standard form, if you would prefer that. I don't have to discuss this case with anyone."

"Oh, that'll do no good," Louise said and stood up. She headed to the kitchen door. "I'll be right back."

I watched her go. She knew more than she was saying. She had an agenda and I wasn't sure what it was.

"What's this about?" Paladin asked.

"You might know more than me," I said.

"All she told me was that the lawyers needed more information because the finances were weird, but it's more than that, isn't it? I thought this would be simple." Paladin said that last bit more to herself than to me.

I couldn't hear anything through those doors. This was part of the servants' wing, back when the rich didn't want their staff to know every little thing. The walls in this building were thick.

"How did you know this wasn't rent-controlled?" Paladin asked.

I had to catch myself from looking at her with surprise. A rent-controlled apartment in the Dakota? I doubted that there had been any since the building became a co-op decades ago.

I would have thought she would know that. But she was based in San Francisco, and she rarely went to East Coast conventions.

Besides, Paladin wasn't the kind of person who understood or was impressed by wealth.

She was waiting for my answer.

"I don't think anything is rent-controlled here," I said trying to be gentle, so as not to insult her intelligence. She was good at what she did, but I was good at what I did, and what I did was figure out nooks and crannies of money, as well as strangeness at science fiction conventions.

"Is that why you asked about ownership?" she asked. "Because I know it wasn't the décor."

"It was partly the décor," I said. "But I'm beginning to figure out the fees on those sheets. One of those fees is the taxes. They're being paid on a quarterly basis."

"So?" Paladin asked.

"So, taxes on this place are probably about two hundred thousand dollars or maybe more, since New York has a mansion tax," I said.

"Two hundred thousand for taxes only?" Paladin asked. She was clearly astonished.

"Taxes only," I said. "Then a place like this will have HOA fees, probably based on square footage and subject to change as the market changes."

The numbers that Paladin had given me didn't make sense for a woman in a rent-controlled apartment, no matter how nice that apartment was. But the numbers snapped into place once I figured out ownership.

"How much would the HOA fees be?" Paladin asked.

"Thousands," I said. I suspected I had seen the fees, and they were actually fifteen thousand, but I didn't want to commit to that. Not yet. "Tens of thousands. This is one of the most desirable buildings in Manhattan, so it'll be a lot."

She frowned. "So...fifty thousand dollars every quarter, and then add more on top of that? Like ten thousand?"

"Or more," I said.

"Jesus," she said. "That's at least twenty-five thousand dollars per month."

She leaned back in her chair. It squeaked—and not a good squeak either. The kind a chair made when it was (forgive the pun) on its last legs.

Then she shook her head. "You'd need a quarter million per year just to break even."

"More than that," I said. "There'd be other fees that would accrue, like some kind of shared building repair or something. And remember, that's just housing. There would be food and clothing and medical expenses..."

My voice trailed off as I thought of those sheets. I wished I had brought them with me now. I could picture them, but I actively wanted to work on them, to see if my assumptions were indeed correct.

"Three hundred thousand?" she asked. "Four hundred? Five?"

I shrugged.

"This isn't making sense," Paladin said.

But it was making sense to me, especially if the aunt was an eccentric. Maybe she was one of those people who didn't like to spend money. Maybe that was what she hoarded, accumulating wealth, and not spending a dime on herself.

Maybe she was reaching an age where she needed to plan her estate, and she had just realized how badly that would hurt her heirs. The estate taxes on this place alone would break them.

Of course, they could probably sell the apartment at a heck of a profit.

And being that kind of hoarder did not explain why she had gotten so huffy about explaining her finances to those lawyers.

Something else was going on.

I saw a shadow near the kitchen door. Louise was coming back.

"She will see you both," Louise said, her voice low. She didn't seem surprised, but she wasn't quite the same. I couldn't put my finger on the difference.

Paladin stood quickly. I took a bit more time, picking up the glass as I hauled myself up.

I set the glass in the sink, which was scratched and scuffed, clearly dating from the 1970s as well. This kitchen was an ancient disaster. Nothing retro here.

I pivoted and followed both Paladin and Louise down the hall. I braced myself for the medicinal smell, but it had faded. Or maybe I had imagined it, or it had simply been a cleaning smell that I misinterpreted.

Louise led us down a narrow hallway that was darker than any other part of the apartment. We went around a sharp corner to find one of those tall mahogany doors.

Louise knocked. A muffled female voice answered. I couldn't make out what she said but Louise clearly heard that as an invitation to go inside.

She pulled the door open and leaned on it. A strong smell of coffee wafted toward us along with the faintly sour smell of a room that rarely got aired out.

Paladin went in first, and stood up straighter as she got inside, which was not the reaction I had expected.

I followed her, expecting to see a small, weak, elderly woman on a bed. Instead, we had entered some kind of office or den.

The room was long and narrow, with a window directly across from the door. Thick, heavy blue curtains, the kind that I hadn't seen for decades, were tied back with gold ropes. An ornate faded rug covered most of the floor, which was a stained wood. A huge fireplace covered the right-hand wall.

The painted patterns on the ceiling matched the rug on the floor. Large, overstuffed chairs were pushed against the wall. They were ancient and antique, clearly part of the room's original design. A floor-to-ceiling painting of a woman covered part of the wall near the window.

But none of that really held my attention. What held my attention was the large partner's desk in the middle of the room. It looked out of place. It was a truly ugly 1980s Chippendale, made of a rosier mahogany than any of the other mahogany in the room. The gold handles on the drawers looked tarnished, and the edges a bit scratched.

The desk didn't surprise me as much as the woman behind it. She was broad-shouldered and appeared tall, although I couldn't quite tell from her position. She had blondish-gray hair that had been in a bun at one point, but that bun had failed its duty hours ago, causing strands of hair to fall about her face.

She didn't look up right away, keeping her attention on the desktop computer screen in front of her. Her hands moved rapidly as she tapped on a Bluetooth keyboard.

Three laptops were open on the desk, as well. A printer sat on a metal TV tray to her right, and papers were scattered all over the desktop in a manner that probably made sense to her.

Finally, she looked up and a shock went through me.

I had met her before.

She blinked and glanced at Louise, then back at me. "Spade?"

"Connie?" I said.

"You *know* her?" Louise asked.

"Spade knows everyone," Paladin said.

I ignored them both and stepped deeper into the room. I was lucky I had pulled Connie's name out of my memory. I hadn't seen her in decades. We had had some great conversations, though, late at night at a couple of East Coast conventions.

By then, she had already forgotten more about mysteries than I had ever known. But she was the one who turned me onto Nero Wolfe, saying I had been misnicknamed.

She had been right.

I went deeper into the room, trying to remember everything I could about her. I'd met so many people over the years, mostly at science fiction conventions, that some got relegated to the back of my memory. Connie had been one of those. I wouldn't have thought of her at all if I hadn't seen her.

She had been a tall, gangly woman back then, slightly pear-shaped, with brown hair that had been cut a lot like her niece's was now—as if she had done it herself. She favored baggy clothes that hid her figure, and she carried a shoulder purse that most of the fannish women refused to carry at a convention.

She had a distracted air even then, and I hadn't been surprised to find out that she had submitted stories to the writing work-shops that every convention hosted.

Like most newbies, she'd been eviscerated by the pros—particularly the newer pros, who hadn't learned how to temper their criticisms with praise. When I found her one night, sitting alone in the café, nursing a hot chocolate and a soggy pastry, that was when I learned her passion was mystery, not science fiction.

But, she had said to me, *there are only two real mystery short fiction markets and a lot of science fiction ones.*

The problem she was having—she thought—was that her sf wasn't that original. I diagnosed a different problem; I thought her problem was that she was too focused on short fiction and she needed to try her hand at a novel.

She sold a mystery novel a year later, and had come to a con—and I couldn't remember which one—to thank me for the advice.

Then the novel came out and sank, as first mysteries were wont to do, and I never saw her again.

Which meant nothing. As I said, I tried not to attend mystery conventions. They weren't—and still aren't—my thing. Too buttoned up for me, with just a little too much emphasis on alcohol.

"God, Spade," Connie said, standing up. She was hunched now—the kind of hunched that people got when they spent too much time at a computer and not enough getting real exercise. "Are you still pretending to be an amateur detective?"

"He's not an amateur," Paladin said. "He is an expert in forensic—"

"I've solved a few cases since we last saw each other," I said, talking over Paladin. I didn't want to spook Connie.

Connie glanced at Paladin, then at me. "You're the person that Louise hired to convince the lawyers that I'm not crazy?"

Paladin glanced sharply at Louise, as if to say, *This is about mental acuity? You didn't tell me.*

"Actually, Louise is on the fence about hiring me," I said, "and I was on the fence about being hired. She hired my friend Paladin here."

"I should have known that someone named Paladin was connected to science fiction." Connie kept her fingertips on the edge of the desk. "You're still Spade, aren't you? You never took me up on Nero Wolfe, did you?"

"I simply read the books after you recommended them," I said. "Unfortunately, I don't have an Archie to do the legwork for me."

She laughed, and so did I. There was an ease between us that had existed from the moment we met; I had forgotten about it.

I turned to Louise and Paladin. "Would you two mind if I talked to Connie alone?"

Paladin half smiled, as if she had been expecting that question since it became clear that Connie and I knew each other. But Louise looked directly at her aunt.

"Aunt Connie," Louise said. "You haven't seen this man in... what, decades? He might have changed. He is a specialist now, in—"

"I'd like to talk with him alone, Louise," Connie said. "Stop worrying about me. I'm fine. And Spade isn't a threat, unless he's *really* changed."

"He's not a threat," Paladin said. "I work with him a lot. He's a good man."

A ringing endorsement from Paladin, but neither of those two women could know that.

"I'm not sure..." Louise said, but Connie made a *pshaw* sound and waved her away. Then she stepped out from behind the desk and grabbed a chair I hadn't seen. It had been hiding behind one of the antique monstrosities. This was a somewhat delicate wooden chair that had seen better days.

I looked at it as if just thinking about sitting in it might destroy it.

"Maybe I'll just stand," I said.

She laughed. "We can use the antiques," she said, "but I warn you. The horsehair is scratchy."

And my legs were tired. They still hadn't recovered from those stairs.

"I'll risk it," I said.

We both walked over to the chairs nearest the window. The curtains, some kind of faded blue velvet, smelled faintly of dust and mildew. I looked at the portrait of the woman, which had probably been on the wall as long as the curtains had been on the window.

The style of the portrait caught my eye, and I couldn't quite believe what I was seeing.

"Is that a John Singer Sargent?" I asked.

"Of my great-grandmother," Connie said. "I liked her. She was a character. The portrait takes liberties. She was never ethereal."

She did look wispy, but so did most of the people in a John Singer Sargeant portrait, which was how I recognized it.

"You're still writing," I said, nodding at the desk, as I sank into the overstuffed chair near great-grandma. Connie was right. The horsehair wasn't just scratchy, it was hard as a rock. The chair was deeply uncomfortable.

Connie frowned at me, almost as if my words had offended her.

So I tried to explain myself. "I hadn't seen anything, not that I read mysteries much. I was looking."

I didn't add that I had looked for a few years, and then stopped looking after a while because I had forgotten.

She glanced at her desk and then shrugged, not meeting my gaze. It was almost as if my comment about her writing had shut down any chance of talking with her.

I'm not usually that bad with people, but I felt like I had blown it here, and I wasn't sure why.

So I decided to switch gears.

"Tell me about the lawyers, Connie," I said. "I'm confused as to why they won't work with you. What am I missing?"

She ran a hand over her mouth, pressing hard, as if she were pushing words back. Then she glanced at the window.

I didn't follow her gaze. I continued watching her, just in case she said something different than I expected.

She tapped her fingers against her lip, then closed her eyes.

"I, um, don't get out much," she said. "My niece worries

about me."

I nodded. "I got that impression."

"I'm fine," she said. "Healthy. But not getting any younger, you know. And I'd been reading about all the changes in taxes, and how the estate tax can break people. I mean, you saw the painting. There are others. And then this apartment. I have no idea the real value. It's high, though, certainly more than my family paid for it decades ago."

Inheritance taxes in New York hit estates worth more than six million. The apartment was probably worth that alone. A John Singer Sargent portrait, signed, would probably add a million all by itself. Not to mention the "others," whatever they were.

So, Connie had a right to worry.

"I made the mistake of telling the lawyers when they were here that the minute I stop working, my money dries up. I mean, I can sell things, but I don't want to." She waved a hand at that painting. "That's my great-grandmother. She belongs here."

I nodded, frowning. I wasn't quite following. Connie was most likely a shut-in, but she worked. And she was living at the edge of her money. I'm not sure why that upset the lawyers.

But she seemed nervous enough that I needed to ask some detailed questions, without upsetting her.

"I'm going to ask a few personal questions," I said. "Feel free to tell me to fuck off."

I don't usually swear like that, except around friends. I still considered Connie a friend, even though we hadn't spoken in decades.

She smiled at my word choice.

"I think I would have told you to fuck off already if I didn't want to have the discussion," she said. The swear word sounded more natural in her mouth than it did in mine.

"All right," I said. "You mentioned your work, and judging by what you were doing, I'm assuming that's writing...?"

Her hand started to move toward her mouth again, but then she seemed to catch herself, bringing her hand down.

"I...um...ghostwrite," she said. "Four books a year."

I frowned. What I knew about writing was that payment was all over the map. Sometimes the writing paid well and sometimes it didn't. She had to have some pretty sweet ghost writing gigs for her to make enough to keep up this place.

"Forgive me," I said. "I didn't see any income marked on those financial sheets."

Her cheeks flushed, and she rubbed her hands on her thighs. This conversation was making her very nervous. Maybe that was what the lawyers saw.

"I—um—the agreement is for expenses, mostly, because they're so high. I want to stay here. But if I stop writing, then there's no more money."

I had never heard of anything like that before, but I refused to be surprised.

"This is through a New York publisher?" I asked.

"Oh, no," she said. "It's a private arrangement."

"With who?" I asked, before I could stop myself.

Her flush grew even deeper. "I can't tell you. I signed a nondisclosure agreement. And I probably said too much already."

"Did you tell the lawyers this?" I asked.

"They wanted to see the agreement," she said. "I can't show it to them. I can't show anyone. And they said that's probably not legal. I should have had a lawyer handle it. But I did. Or we did, when it was put together."

"We?" I asked.

"Me and...you know...the person I'm writ—the other person."

"You shared a lawyer," I said.

She nodded, still looking down. "You don't have to yell at me.

The lawyers already did. They said I should have had my own lawyer. But I was sad and I thought I would eventually lose this place, so I did it all fast."

She took a deep breath, and then her hand came back up, rubbing her mouth again.

"I don't mind, really. It's a good deal and people read my work, even though they don't see my name. But that's just like a pen name, so it's not a big deal. It's just a problem for the estate."

My mind was churning. I thought it was a problem in a variety of ways, but I wasn't going to jump in like that. Not yet.

"Why is it a problem for the estate?" I asked.

"If I die tomorrow, the payments stop," she said. "I don't want anything to be sold. I was going to have that in the trust. Not the valuable stuff like the paintings. They *belong* here."

That was a different issue, and one I'd seen a million times. People tried to control an estate from beyond the grave. It never worked out well.

"I wanted everything in the trust for my niece and nephews. We—me and the lawyers—were setting it up so that the family would all need to agree to sell a piece of the estate. They were explaining how hard it would all be, but then we started talking about the finances and the lawyers wanted to know how it all worked and one of them, the young one, he suggested that maybe we sell just one painting or maybe my grandmother's jewelry and set the money inside the trust to handle any financial issues until everything could get settled after I died and—"

She looked up at me, her eyes lined with tears.

"—I can't sell any of that. It belongs in the family. It *has* to stay here." She cleared her throat. "So I asked them to leave."

I wasn't sure why this was so fraught for her. But I can be a good listener when I wanted to be, and I was listening now.

"Before they did, the young one, he said, no one would know

if he saw the nondisclosure, and I said *I* would know, and then he said none of this sounded like it was aboveboard because he'd done some publishing things, and no one worked for expenses, ever. That was just weird, and maybe illegal."

The young one had to know that this wasn't illegal per se if there was a valid contract. Did he know something I didn't?

Probably.

"Because you didn't have a contract?" I asked.

"Oh, the nondisclosure is part of the contract," she said, as if I already knew that.

"That a lawyer shared by you and this other person drew up," I said.

"That's not illegal," she said. "And it was a long time ago. Expenses here have gone up dramatically. They always get paid."

"But that's all you're getting," I said.

"And, you know, some extra for food and such," she said a bit defensively.

"Which is a regular expense," I said.

Her lips thinned.

"You ghostwrite books for a famous person, then," I said.

She tilted her head. "Spade, you know I can't tell you that."

"But the person was famous when they hired you," I said.

She considered the question, maybe comparing it in her mind to the nondisclosure.

"I can't," she said.

"Does the other person live up to the nondisclosure?" I asked.

She let out a small laugh. "Are you sure you're not a lawyer?" she asked. "Because the young one asked the same thing."

I waited. If the other person had violated the nondisclosure, it was breached and Connie could tell me what was going on.

Because my spidey sense was tingling big time. Clearly the lawyer's had been too.

"And no, the other person hasn't violated it, and I doubt they ever will. It's not in their best interest to do so." She sat up, primly almost.

"Because they're passing off your work as theirs," I said.

"That's what ghostwriting is, Spade." She gave me an odd sideways look. "I thought you knew that. It's not illegal."

"No," I said, feeling deeply disturbed. "It's not."

"The suggestion for a detective was facetious," she said. "That young lawyer, he said if he discovered who the other party was without me telling him, that didn't violate the agreement. So he said we should just hire a detective to figure it out. Unfortunately, Louise took him seriously."

"Law firms have their own detectives, Connie," I said, hoping I didn't sound too condescending. "They could have hired someone if they wanted to. There didn't have to be all this subterfuge."

"I know that," Connie said. "But tell Louise. She was irritated —heck *I* was irritated that they don't want to do the trust because of me. They don't know if the nondisclosure transfers to the estate or dies with me, and they can't know because I won't show them the contract."

She sat up and gave me a plaintive look.

"Spade," she said, "I *can't* show anyone the agreement, not without violating it."

Which isn't suspicious at all, I wanted to say, but I didn't, mostly because she seemed very vulnerable right now.

"We're at an impasse, and I'm aware of the fact that the impasse is me." She rubbed her hands together, as if she was trying to keep them away from her mouth. "I suppose it would just be easier to sell something."

"It would be easier to let your lawyers look at the nondisclosure and that contract," I said.

170

She shook her head. "I can't, Spade. I've been doing this for years. I expect to do it for years more. I don't want to damage a sure thing."

"But you let your niece hire a detective," I said.

"I told her that she *couldn't* hire a detective," Connie said. "When she told me about this Paladin person, your friend, I said I didn't want to talk to her. I guess Louise gave her the financial documents I gave to the lawyers. And now you're here. But I'm not hiring you, Spade. There's no reason to. I know what's going on."

Connie did too. It was a mess, one I didn't like at all, just like that lawyer.

"Can I ask another question?" I asked.

She smiled a little, showing her fannish roots. "You just did."

"You know what I mean," I said.

"I do," she said. "Ask away. I can't answer you."

"Are you getting any royalties on these books?" I asked.

"You haven't been following publishing, have you, Spade?" she asked. "No one gets royalties anymore."

I knew that wasn't true. I knew dozens of authors, big names in particular, who got royalties and had throughout their careers. I also knew that publishing was changing and newer writers who went into traditional publishing—*New York* publishing—rarely if ever got royalties. These things were always big topics of conversation at conventions...and at places like the Edgar Awards.

"I guess I don't know publishing, then," I said, trying to be as disingenuous as possible. "How long has this been going on?"

"Oh, my goodness," she said, waving her right hand dismissively. "As long as I've been in the business. My first novel—you know, you read it—never earned out. Most novels, even the big ones, don't. The deals are structured so that the writer gets all the money in the advance, and the publisher keeps the rest."

I had to work hard to keep my expression impassive. Yes, many deals were structured so that writers got their money up front because New York publishers tried to predict sales. But readers were almost impossible to predict, and books took off like rockets, often unexpectedly.

People earned royalties all the time. *Writers* earned royalties all the time.

Someone was lying to her.

"I'm pretty lucky to get what I'm getting," she said. I suspected she was parroting words someone else had told her.

"What does your agent say about all of this?" I asked.

She smiled at me. "I haven't needed an agent in decades. I get my own deals."

Worse and worse. I didn't like agents, but sometimes they could be useful.

"So you haven't tried to sell one of your original novels in years, then," I said, not really asking a question. Just thinking about the quirky and dark voice that had disappeared from the mystery genre.

"These are my originals," she said, and then clapped a hand over her mouth. Her eyes grew wide. She knew she had misspoken.

"You mean the people you ghost for don't give you an outline? A suggestion of what to do?"

She looked at the painting of her great-grandmother as if the long-dead woman could help her.

"Is this actually spelled out in the nondisclosure?" I asked. "If not, you can tell me."

She closed her eyes for a moment, then dropped her hand, and rubbed her legs again. I wanted to catch her fingers, and stop all of the nervous gestures.

"The nondisclosure only discusses what happens after the

book is turned in," she said quietly. "My partn—um, the people I work for—they trust me to come up with the right kind of material, as long as it's in the correct genre, the one we started in."

"Mystery," I said.

She nodded, but didn't look at me.

I was seething and I wasn't exactly sure how to hide it. Someone—or several someones—was passing Connie's work off as their own. I knew that was common in ghostwriting, but there was supposed to be some kind of ethics there. The person whose name was on the cover should have participated in some way—either with an idea or an outline or a discussion or even approving all of the material as it went along.

And ghostwriters always went through publishers or agents, as far as I knew. The really unusual ones were for the mega bestsellers who had health issues or were slowly fading into dementia, but were too big a cash cow to let them slide into oblivion.

Then a ghostwriter got hired to mimic the writer's voice and stories. Often that person worked off an existing outline or a direction set down by the original writer or the editor.

I'd never heard of anything like this before.

"If you didn't work with an agent or an editor," I said, "how did this all start?"

She looked at me, alarmed, as if I was asking her to break a dozen laws.

"And any time you veer too close to something you can't disclose," I said, "just swerve away."

I was pretty sure that the origins of this mess weren't included in those agreements, but I was just guessing.

"You were there, Spade," she said. "Don't you remember?"

"I was?" I asked.

"My last convention," she said. "I was crying. You told me not to give up."

I blinked, thought, then remembered. That panel, an up-and-coming writers panel, led by an editor who is now fortunately deceased. The man was unpleasant on good days, terrible and nasty on bad ones.

He'd been having a bad day and unfortunately, he got to moderate that panel.

He wouldn't let Connie talk because she was a mystery writer, and they were at an sf convention. I had come to the panel to support Connie and a couple of other friends. I knew that he was an asshole, and I knew that they were in for a rough time.

The problem—well, I caused it. Because the panel was nearly over, and except for introducing herself in a quiet voice, and holding up the paperback of her first novel, which was sliding out of print as she did so, Connie had said nothing on the panel.

The four sf writers—all men, one of whom had only published a short story (albeit a highly acclaimed one)—had gone on at length. But she sat there quietly, patiently, waiting for a turn that wasn't going to come.

So stupid me, I raised my hand and said that I liked mysteries and I would like to hear about Connie's book.

I can tell you about her book, asshole editor said. *It's overrated and poorly written. She's one of those writers whose career has ended before it ever started.*

Connie sat bolt upright, as if she had been struck in the face. One of the sf writers, an older man who would go on to have a bit more success than the others, said, *That's unduly harsh, David*, to the editor, and at that moment, a member of the concom entered the room and held up a sign, telling the panel they had gone overtime.

The panel broke up without another word. Connie grabbed her paperback and fumbled her way off the dais.

I met her in the aisle. Her lower lip was trembling. *We need to get out of here, Spade,* she said, and pushed past me.

I followed her to one of those little nooks that some hotels had, an arrangement of furniture that faced a window or a wall. In this case, the arrangement—a couch and two chairs—faced a group of potted palms. I remembered that because I stared at them while Connie sobbed against me, telling me over and over again that she had been found out.

Every writer feared that. In my experience, every writer was a complicated mix of insecurity and overconfidence, and it took very little to let the insecurity win.

Don't give up, I told her. *He's one man, and not your editor. He works in science fiction, and he's known for destroying his writers. Your editor loves you.*

And can't buy my next book, Connie said. *Not unless I change my name because my name doesn't have good sales.*

So change your name, I said. *What matters is that you write.*

Damn, damn, and double damn. I had said that. Whose clutches had I sent her into?

Whoever it was, they were smart enough to figure out a way to prevent her from telling me. From telling anyone.

"So...someone else heard about that awful panel," I said.

She shrugged, still looking down.

"Not an editor," I said, poking one last time.

"No, not an editor," she said. "Someone who actually likes my work."

And if they were at that convention so long ago, then I knew them. Or at least knew of them. Had met them, at least once.

"That's when they hired you to write their books," I said.

She looked at me, biting her lower lip.

"Someone famous," I said.

Her head shook just enough before she caught herself. Then she ran her hand over her mouth. The nervous gestures were back.

"You know," she said after a moment, "there's this theory that the problem with getting your books to readers is a marketing problem, not a writing problem."

I'd heard that. I also knew it wasn't true. I'd seen hundreds of heavily hyped books that died awful deaths. As I said, readers are unpredictable. They like what they like, whether there's a huge marketing push behind it or not.

"And the theory goes," she said, "that if the right person—a talented person—handles the marketing, a really good book will get to readers. It'll get read like it's supposed to."

God, she had been vulnerable at that convention. And needy. And open to a suggestion like that.

"So you took my advice," I said, voice low. "You put a different name on your books."

"Ghostwriting," she said. "All of the fun of writing and none of the nasty work with publishers, editors, and marketing departments. Just a daily word count and a lot of imagination."

It sounded perfect, except for the fact that the money seemed odd. Beyond odd.

"You know, I had a small cash inheritance," she said. "In addition to this place. I had income. And that gave me time to build the ghostwriting business, which has paid off."

Then her expression clouded. "Except now. I am not sure how to deal with the lawyers and the estate."

I nodded. Half of my brain was busy trying to figure out who the con artist was and the other half was dealing with extreme regret. And a bit of a worry. Connie's entire life had been built that afternoon when that hideous editor, fortunately now dead, had eviscerated a vulnerable writer in front of an audience of maybe twenty people all for the sake of his own petty little ego.

"See why we don't need a detective, Spade?" she asked.

"I do," I said. "I really do."

2

I left her office maybe fifteen minutes later. I did manage to clarify one thing: the people we were discussing—the ones who made her sign that contract with the nondisclosure—did not live in this building.

That ruled out a really big-name mystery writer. I had already ruled him out anyway, since, to my knowledge, he had never gone to sf conventions. But sometimes my knowledge was limited, especially on random attendees before they became someone famous.

I like to brag about my steel-trap memory, but when it comes to conventions, the memory doesn't work as well as I would like. Conventions, to me, are one big convention that has gone on for decades. I might be able to pinpoint an event by year or by location, but I cannot figure out who was where when because conversations and amoeba tables and programming blend together, as if the convention goes on and I'm the only thing that changes.

So I had to do some research, because I knew research would quiet my mind.

I was contemplating all of that when I entered the kitchen. Paladin and Louise were sitting at the table. Paladin stood when I came in.

"Did you figure out what's going on?" she asked.

"Yeah, maybe," I said.

"Oh, good," she said. "So this is solved."

Louise was clutching a cup of tea that was mostly finished. Paladin's was sitting in front of her chair, untouched. There were some Mrs. Fields's bite-sized cookies in a branded container in the center of the table. One half-eaten cookie sat on a napkin near

Paladin's tea. Apparently Paladin, who had a heck of a sweet tooth, wasn't that fond of Mrs. Fields.

I wanted to grab all of the cookies and shove them in my mouth. Eating my stress, which was why I sometimes had issues with stairs.

"No," I said. "Not—not solved."

Louise's face fell. "So what, we just live with the situation? And there will be no trust?"

I looked at her. I still hadn't quite figured her out. Did she want the place to herself? Was she truly someone who helped her aunt? Or was Louise someone who wanted to control everything?

Because I didn't know, I wasn't going to say very much.

"Help your aunt figure out what to sell, so that there's extra money in the trust to handle expenses for a few years while you and your siblings make decisions," I said.

I sounded harsh. I wasn't sure I meant to.

Louise frowned at me. "The lawyers said that too. But you talked to my aunt for an hour. You know she doesn't want to do that."

"And the rest of this is too big a mess to be easily solved," I said. "If you want that trust set up in the next year or so, you'll need to sell something."

Paladin frowned at me. She wasn't the most diplomatic person —heck, she wasn't even the most diplomatic one of the two of us —but she wasn't used to me being quite this blunt.

"Spade," she said. "You want to tell us what you discussed?"

"No," I said, and headed for the door.

I heard Paladin apologizing behind me, which was impressive in and of itself. Paladin didn't usually apologize either, not for someone else's behavior.

I let myself out and faced those damn stairs. Maybe I would

take the elevator. I just wanted to get out of the building, and return to my computers. That's where the answers were.

Paladin reached me a moment later. She ushered me toward the stairs.

"What was that all about?" she asked.

I grabbed the polished railing and started down the stairs. "Do you happen to know who Connie is working with?"

I had had a suspicion from the start that Paladin knew what exactly was going on, but wanted me to ferret it all out in case there was a court case.

Paladin did not go to court if she could avoid it, and good lawyers didn't want her on the stand. Paladin stretched too many rules to be an effective witness—on anything.

"No," she said. "I don't have any idea."

I was getting close to the bottom of the stairs. I had gone faster than I usually did, mostly because I wanted to get out of here.

"But you wanted to come during the Edgars," I said.

"Maybe I'm a mystery fan," she said.

I gave her a withering look. "Paladin."

She sighed, and passed me, reaching the bottom before me.

"I just figured, you know, that we'd have to talk with a bunch of people in mystery publishing and the Edgar ceremony was the best way to do it without drawing attention to anything."

I stared at her. Of course it was. That was the Paladin I knew. Somewhat devious and always thinking ahead.

"Okay," I said.

"Did I figure wrong?" she asked.

"I don't know yet," I said.

"She's being screwed, Spade, you know that," Paladin said.

"Yep, but a lot of people get screwed, Paladin. I'm willing to bet that she signed a legal contract."

"Without benefit of an attorney," Paladin said.

"Well, there was an attorney." I stepped past her and went to the exit. A doorman stood just outside. I wondered if he was waiting for us, or if the poor man had to stand in the courtyard every minute of every day.

"But not a good one," Paladin said.

"Look," I said. "The only legal way to resolve this would be if Connie let someone see the agreement and we figure out who she's working with. Then, if the contract is aboveboard, she'd have to go to equity court, which might be the right thing to do. But it would take time and money, and I'm not sure this estate has either."

"She's dying?" Paladin asked. "I didn't think she was dying."

"Cases like this," I said, trying not to use my didactic voice, "can take a decade or more."

"Oh," Paladin said. "So there's nothing we can do."

We walked past those fragrant lilies of the valley. Their sweet smell wasn't as pleasing as it had been earlier.

"I'm not sure yet," I said. "I need to figure a few things out first."

"Okay," she said, then ran ahead of me to get a cab.

3

It took research and several phone calls, lots of downloads, and the help of a few SMoFs to get everything I needed. SMoFs are the Secret Masters of Fandom, of whom I am one. We're the people who run conventions. Most folk who attend don't know our names or even what we do, but we keep track of everything.

It's just harder when the convention took place before everyone uploaded every bit of their lives—first to some website (back in the day) and then to social media.

I had to pinpoint that old convention, which was hard enough. That took a bit of digging. I needed the publication date of Connie's first novel which was, apparently, not available in ebook and was nearly sold out in paper versions.

People liked it and remembered it and wanted to keep it, even if they believed she never wrote anything else.

Once I had the publication date, I needed to figure out where those potted palms were. It wasn't New York, although the asshole editor's presence narrowed things down considerably. He went to some East Coast conventions, Readercons, World Fantasy Cons, the award-based cons like the Nebulas (which this was not, because back in the day there wasn't that kind of programming), and a handful of fannish conventions where he was the Guest of Honor.

After his assholery became really clear, his GoH stints dried up, and my memory suggested that was *before* this incident. I wasn't sure, though. It took about two hours to figure out that the incident in question had taken place at a Los Angeles Westercon, back in the day when *Locus*, the main trade magazine of science fiction, was handing out its awards at a ceremony there.

That explained why asshole editor had been there, and it also explained the potted palms. It did not explain why Connie had been there, and I was not about to ask. Sometimes, in the early years of their careers, writers went to as many big conventions as possible to have face time with editors.

Or, for all I know, the Westercon appearance had been part of a self-organized book tour, trying to bump up her sales numbers and probably failing spectacularly.

I certainly wasn't going to ask.

The con was far enough back that the computerized list of attendees would probably have been stored on some kind of external device—a hard drive, a disk, a thumb drive. And the paper list of attendees was probably in a box in the basement of a SMoF somewhere in the greater Los Angeles area.

Which meant I needed photos and for that I had to go to some of the sf field's unofficial photographers. People like Jay Kay Klein took thousands of photographs over decades. I hoped I wouldn't have to get into anything he had done, because I would have had to contact the library at the University of California Riverside which held his collection.

That would slow me down. But there were half a dozen other unofficial photographers and I contacted the ones who owed me favors first.

Not everyone had been at that Westercon. It took a while to find a trove of photographs, and even longer to convince the photographers to give me access to their online storage for their scanned photos.

But it all paid off. Not only did I find pictures of that awful panel (with a serious-looking me in the back of the room), but I also found what I considered to be the most important image.

Connie was wearing the same clothes, her face blotchy and red, sitting alone in the small hotel café. In the next few shots, a man had joined her. At first, I didn't recognize him because the pictures only showed the back of his head. Clearly the photographer had been interested in Connie, not him.

Then he turned sideways and I might have audibly gasped. I recognized him.

Hell, the entire world would recognize him.

That was Rory Wright, long before he was famous, when he was a beanpole of a man, instead of the buff gym-muscled creature he had become. In the picture, he was wearing chinos and a button-down white shirt with the sleeves rolled up, showing off his scrawny arms.

He appeared to be talking seriously with Connie and judging by the three photographs of her face, she was listening intently.

I had vague memories of Wright, but not from that convention. From a Worldcon a few years later, when he demanded to be put on programming. I hadn't been running programming, and was pointing him to the right person, when he went off on me.

Don't you know who I am? You people are lucky to have me here. I bring my own following.

I have always hated entitled celebrities, which Wright was by then. I had said to him, *Then take your following to the bar. If there's room on programming, I'm sure someone will be in touch with you.*

He had stopped coming to conventions shortly after that. Or sf conventions anyway. As I've said, I don't go to mystery conventions.

But I had read a few of his books. They were surprisingly heartfelt and intuitive. In particular, his female characters were strong and capable, with more depth than I saw from a lot of his male colleagues.

I wasn't the only person who found his writing compelling. His books sold in the millions of copies and had for years. Several of his stand-alone titles had been made into movies. One of his major series had become a network television show, back when that meant something. I'd just read that he'd sold a few more projects to streaming services.

Then there were the board games and merchandise and a whole bunch of things I'd never seen in the mystery field. Wright had become a force, not just as a writer, but as a marketer. And he was the go-to guy for media outlets if they needed a writer to discuss something literary or even something tangentially related to his work.

While he was an ass in person, he was a heck of an interview.

I had always wondered how he had time to maintain his fiefdom and write at least four books per year, occasionally more. I just figured he was thin and athletic, which meant he probably had five times the energy I did.

I had figured a lot of things that I was beginning to realize were wrong.

I looked at that photograph of Wright before he was famous, sitting with Connie, who thought her life and career and dreams had ended, and I felt a wave of antipathy that I hadn't felt in a long time.

Then I made myself breathe. I couldn't make assumptions. I needed knowledge.

Fortunately, I had the skills to acquire that knowledge quickly.

4

Well, somewhat quickly. I stayed in my room for hours, digging into the materials that Louise had given Paladin. Fortunately there were bank printouts as well as tax information from the State of New York itself. I set aside Connie's tax returns and focused instead on the payment records that I had at my fingertips.

I was so preoccupied that I barely noticed that Paladin had brought me pizza, until the smell made me remember I was in New York, where all pizzas were perfect, even the ones bought from some streetside vendor (which this was not).

I ate and worked and occasionally grunted—at least that was what Paladin told me later. She came in and out, asked me questions I didn't even seem to hear, and then went about her business whatever it was.

I had thought the search would be easy. I had the tools, after all. But I had run into a wall of corporate shell companies. The company that paid the taxes was different from the company that paid for the apartment which was different from the company that gave Connie her expenses.

I couldn't make assumptions either, because that would taint the work. So I had to trace the corporate registrations until I found a mistake. It was hard to find one, because these corporations were registered in states with tight corporate shield laws.

But thank god for the Brits. Some scandal a few years back made them clean up their corporate secrecy laws to get rid of a cottage industry of money launderers. Companies House, the UK's company registration agency, was forcing every corporation on its books to not only name a company's directors, but investigate whether or not the names and addresses were false.

The corporation three layers up from the corporation that paid for Connie's expenses had originally been registered in the UK, and slapped with some kind of fine for a lack of transparency —partly because the corporation had been improperly dissolved, but not before someone launched an investigation of the entire enterprise.

Apparently there were so many shell companies (all US-based) attached to this one corporation that the officials in the UK thought this was a money laundering scheme. Instead, it was a tax avoidance scheme that didn't pay off. The company—and its sole director, one Rory Wright—had to pay fines equivalent to six years' worth of British taxes.

I didn't read the full report to see all the machinations. I didn't need to.

I had the information I needed.

I just wasn't sure what to do with it.

Rory Wright was worth, according to a *Forbes* estimate based on publicly known deals, at least $80 million. Eighty million buys a lot of attorneys.

Even if Connie's lawyers went after him for a tiny bit of that money, the case would be tied up in court forever. And the publicity would make that comment from the asshole editor seem like child's play.

Most commentators, all of whom knew Wright, and none of whom knew Connie, would say that she was a failed writer who just wanted attention. I could see everything play out, and it would be bad for Connie even if she got the money.

I wondered if she knew how much Wright was worth. I wondered if she knew how popular he was as a personality. If she did, her adamant reaction to following the nondisclosure agreement made even more sense.

As I finished, Paladin came back into the room with a Diet

Coke for me and another pizza. Apparently, I'd been working longer than I had thought.

"Bad news?" she asked.

"I'm not sure yet," I said.

Paladin set down the pizza. It was an old-fashioned sausage and mushroom pizza, with a crust so thin that the grease had already seeped into the box. Absolutely perfect.

Paladin grabbed a slice. "You're going to tell me what's going on, though, right?"

"Yeah," I said. "I need to do some out-loud thinking."

Paladin gave me a half smile. "Happy to be your sounding board," she said.

5

Sounding board and investigator. She was the one who found Rory Wright for me. Her strategy of coming to the Edgars paid off.

Wright was supposed to present The Best Episode of a TV Series Edgar on Thursday night, and rehearsals were the day before. Which meant he was already in the city, somewhere.

I was going to comb hotel registrations or maybe try to run into him at the open bar at the Edgars, but Paladin had seen him two mornings in a row. Apparently, he favored the same diner we had discovered, only he was one of the writers who had moved to that room in the back.

I was unusually nervous that morning. If I did this wrong, I could hurt the equilibrium that Connie had maintained for a very long time. But I also couldn't let it go.

Paladin had smiled at me when I said that to her. We both were the kind of people who couldn't walk away from an injustice.

I just got angrier at financial ones than she did.

We went to the diner early. Paladin searched the inside while I waited outside. It was a deliciously cool morning, promising a beautiful spring day ahead. People were walking to work, and there weren't a lot of tourists out yet. They were probably all sleeping in.

I had one of my laptops under my arm. I tried not to shift from foot to foot as I waited. Paladin came back out and shook her head.

I told her to go in and get herself something to eat. We would switch off. If we didn't see Wright here, I would either search hotel registries or I would tell him I needed to talk with him when we got to the Edgars.

I would have to work my own magic to get inside, because neither Paladin nor I had invitations to the ceremony.

But we didn't need them. Paladin came out just as I saw Wright ambling down the sidewalk. He didn't come from our hotel. He came from a side street that had a few luxury rentals which I had looked at before we came.

"I got this," I said to Paladin.

She didn't argue. She went back inside to order breakfast.

Fortunately, Wright was alone. He had reached the entrance to my hotel. I walked over to him, clutching my laptop tightly.

He was shorter than I am, but not by much. He actually spent his money on expensive clothing, although it was still chinos and a cleanly pressed white shirt. Just a more expensive version of the outfit he had worn all those years ago.

"Rory," I said.

He looked over at me, then a condescending smile crossed his face. "If it isn't Spade, the pretend detective."

I almost snapped back, *If it isn't Rory Wright, the pretend writer*, but I couldn't let my antipathy get the better of me right now.

"I need to talk with you," I said.

"Researching your first book?" he asked in that same tone.

"About Connie," I said.

He blinked, as if the name didn't register. For a brief half second, I wondered if I had gotten this all wrong.

Then he raised his chin and said, "I don't feel like talking to you," and I knew.

"You need to talk with me," I said. "Let's go inside."

He looked at the diner longingly, but I steered him into the hotel. I bought us both coffee at the Starbucks. Mine was normal, with cream and sugar. His was some kind of specialty something or other that took a bit of negotiation to figure out.

He grabbed a banana as well, and then we sat in a nook far from the elevators. If there had been potted palms, I would have come full circle, but there weren't. Just a few ugly iron sculptures that twisted their way toward the ceiling.

I set my phone between us. Wright didn't even look at it, which was good, because I had already pressed *record*. In New York, it only took one party to consent for a recording to be allowed in court.

I doubted he knew that.

"Before you say anything," I said, "I need to tell you that I was hired in my capacity as a forensic accountant by Connie's family to figure out what is going on with her finances. She won't talk to anyone, citing a contract and a nondisclosure agreement that she plans to honor until she dies."

He watched me. To his credit, he didn't say, *I have no idea what this has to do with me.*

I told him about the financial trail he had left, and he shrugged.

"Taking care of a friend, is all," he said, which was an admittance, and more than I needed, really.

But I still had to tread carefully.

I opened my laptop and showed him the pictures that I had gotten of that long-ago convention. I also showed him photos of the conversation, a handshake that I had found later, and a scrawled piece of paper that I suspected was the first draft of their partnership agreement.

"So?" he asked.

"So, you have an equity issue, Rory," I said.

His fingers played with his coffee cup, but his gaze remained on me. "Equity."

"She's writing your books," I said. "She's done so from the beginning. Back then, you paid a good fee. But now you're worth millions. You need to pay her more."

"This is extortion," he said.

"This is about fairness," I said. "And if it goes to the court, which it might, because the family is trying to protect their assets as Connie ages, a judge could compel her to present that contract. It would probably be under seal, but the secret would be out."

His eyes narrowed. He looked meaner than I remembered. Then he shook his head.

"It's so upsetting when a disgruntled fan tries to take credit for my work," he said. "It's worse when the fan is a failed writer."

I closed my laptop. "If that's how you want to play it," I said, "but you need to understand something. The contract won't protect you forever."

He frowned just enough for me to know that I had hooked him.

"There's a quirk in the copyright law," I said. "After thirty-five years, the original writer can petition to get all the rights back to her work. It's granted automatically. So if Connie can prove the work is hers, and she probably can, then she'll be able to publish your old novels as hers. You are coming up on thirty-five years, aren't you?"

His expression didn't change, but his skin paled as if all the blood was fleeing.

"That can't be true," he said after a minute.

Gotcha, asshole, I thought. Instead, I said, "It is. Check with an intellectual property attorney. If I were you, Rory, I'd get ahead of this. A lot of music studios are finally paying back payments and a new royalty share to the musicians they screwed for decades to prevent exactly this. I think you might want to do the same."

Then I picked up my laptop and tucked it under my arm. I

grabbed my phone, careful not to shut off the recording and spoke very slowly. "As I said, I don't work for Connie. She has kept your secret. I haven't seen the contract that you have, if there is a contract. I know there's a nondisclosure because that's why the lawyers for the family hired me. They wanted to know if I could figure out who was on the other side of the nondisclosure. I have."

"You're a fabulist, Spade," Rory said. "No reputable law firm would hire you."

I reached into my pocket and pulled out my wallet. From there, I removed my business card with my real name on it. I set the card on the table in front of him.

"I testify all over the country in my role as a forensic financial analyst. I've been hired by nearly a hundred different law firms for many different cases." I grinned at him, even though I didn't feel like grinning. "You might want to look me up."

Then I walked away, my heart pounding. I might have ruined the delicate balance that Connie had maintained for years. Or I might have given her and her family more money than they could ever imagine.

I went outside and immediately walked into the diner. Paladin was finishing a gigantic plate of French toast at the table we'd had the day before.

"Call those attorneys," I said quietly. "We need to meet immediately."

"Why?" she asked.

"Because I need to be on their payroll by end of day," I said. "Tell them I solved their trust fund problem."

"But...?" she asked, recognizing my tone.

"I might have made things worse."

6

I didn't exactly make things worse, but only because we acted quickly. I met with the attorneys, they hired me at my usual fee, and I explained what I found. I made them promise to keep this close without telling Louise or her siblings who was behind the nondisclosures, at least until the case against Wright was underway.

I haven't seen lawyers salivate before. They saw the money, they saw Rory Wright, they saw my proof—and oh, they listened to the recording. They were seeing dollar signs. Millions of dollar signs.

I gave them advice, though. I told them to keep all of this out of the press, or the case would take years to resolve.

"Rory doesn't want anyone to know that he didn't write a single word," I said. "He'll pay a lot of money to keep that quiet... if you handle this right."

Part of handling it right was to approach him with a new contract. But I couldn't do that. I couldn't do anything else.

I couldn't even go apologize to Connie for meddling in her business because, if her attorneys did this right, she wouldn't know until the new contract landed on her desk.

I didn't want to be there for the fallout of that.

As I was leaving, one of the attorneys—the young one, the one that Connie had thought was a thorn in her side—stopped me.

"I think we should talk Connie into writing books under her own name," he said. "You're the one who got through to her, enough that we could figure this out."

I didn't like the *we* when *I* was the one who figured this out. But I let him talk.

"I know some people in publishing, but I'll wager you know more. If she publishes a book of her own—"

"She'll never make the same kind of money," I said.

"But it's her storytelling that made this work," he said.

I shook my head. "It was a confluence of events," I said. "It takes a long time to build a name, like Rory Wright has. They did —they do—have a partnership. And from what I can tell, Connie is happy with it. She's a shut-in. She's not going to be able to do anything akin to the promotion that Rory does."

And besides, I didn't say, the world was different now. Building a brand name in a world filled with noise was hard.

"Focus on getting her what's owed to her," I said.

"You never told us what is owed to her," he said.

I looked at him. "You did go to law school, right?"

He flushed. "Yes."

"Then you know. What's owed to her is what you people can negotiate, without blowing the deal."

And then I walked away.

From the whole thing.

Forever.

I didn't have to testify in any court. I never saw any whisper of the fact that Rory Wright didn't write a word of his novels.

And Paladin told me that the trust for the estate got finished within six months.

"Before," Paladin told me, "anyone in the family knew what kind of money was involved."

I was really glad I hadn't been there for that family meeting.

I hate estate work, and I'd gotten roped into this one. Estate work always makes me feel like a true golden age detective, only one who didn't really care if Aunt Mabel stole the silver before someone kiboshed her with the Ming vase from the library.

I didn't like those books. I prefer science fiction in my mysteries, rather like peanut butter in my chocolate.

Which was why Paladin and I avoided the big Edgar ceremony on Thursday night. Instead, we went to the diner and slid into the back, sharing a gigantic piece of cheesecake like two teenagers on a date.

We were not on a date. Paladin and I did not date.

But when we worked together, it was absolute magic.

And I would take that, any day of the week.

New York Times Bestselling Author

KRISTINE KATHRYN
RUSCH

Spade
Paladin

THE EARLY
CONUNDRUMS

A Spade/Paladin Collection

If you enjoyed Assorted Conundrums, *you might also like the Spade/Paladin short story collection* The Early Conundrums. *Available from wmgbooks.com or your favorite bookseller.*

Follow Kris on BookBub!

I value honest feedback, and would love to hear your opinion in a review, if you're so inclined, on your favorite book retailer's site.

Be the first to know!

Just sign up for the Kristine Kathryn Rusch newsletter, and keep up with the latest news, releases and so much more—even the occasional giveaway.

So, what are you waiting for? To sign up go to kriswrites.com.

But wait! There's more. Sign up for the WMG Publishing newsletter, too, and get the latest news and releases from all of the WMG authors and lines, including Kristine Grayson, Kris Nelscott, Dean Wesley Smith, *Pulphouse Fiction Magazine,* and so much more.

To sign up go to wmgpublishing.com.

ABOUT THE AUTHOR

An international bestseller with more than 35 million books sold, Kristine Kathryn Rusch writes in many genres, from mystery to science fiction, from western to romance. Most of her work appears as Kristine Kathryn Rusch, while her Kris Nelscott pen name is highly acclaimed, and her Kristine Grayson pen name became a bestseller in romance. Her science fiction novels set in the bestselling Diving Universe have won dozens of awards and are in development for a major TV show. She also writes the Retrieval Artist sf series and several major series that mostly appear as short fiction.

Her novels have made bestseller lists around the world and her short fiction has appeared in twenty-seven best-of-the-year collections. She has won more than thirty awards for her fiction, including the *Ellery Queen Mystery Magazine* Readers Award, the Hugo, *Le Prix Imaginales*, and the *Asimov's* Readers' Award. Publications from *The Chicago Tribune* to *Booklist* have included her Kris Nelscott mystery novels in their top-ten-best mystery novels of the year. The Nelscott books have received nominations for almost every award in the mystery field, including the best novel Edgar Award, and the Shamus Award.

To keep up with everything she does, go to kriswrites.com and sign up for her newsletter. To track her many pen names and series, see their individual websites (krisnelscott.com, kristinegrayson.com, retrievalartist.com, divingintothewreck.com, pulphousemagazine.com, wmgholidayspectacular.com).

facebook.com/kristinekathrynruschwriter

patreon.com/kristinekathrynrusch

bookbub.com/authors/kristine-kathryn-rusch